"Come in."

Alain's voice was curt as he continued. "Let's get this over with, shall we? And I might as well make it clear that this evening was definitely *not* my idea."

Roxanne squared her shoulders and stepped inside. "I thought my presence didn't bother you in the least," she retorted. "Isn't that what you told me?"

"Yes. But although I can understand my parents inviting you—for politeness' sake—I find it inappropriate for you to be here."

The harsh directness of his voice hurt, but she stood her ground. "Why on earth didn't you say so earlier? I'm sure if we'd put our heads together, we could have dreamed up a way out."

He laughed humorlessly. "We don't escape our sins that easily, I'm afraid. There's always a price to pay."

Lee Stafford was born and educated in Sheffield, where she worked as a secretary and in public relations. Her husband is in hospital catering management. They live in Sussex with their two teenage daughters.

Books by Lee Stafford

SUMMER'S ECHO
Lee Stafford

Harlequin Books

TORONTO • NEW YORK • LONDON
AMSTERDAM • PARIS • SYDNEY • HAMBURG
STOCKHOLM • ATHENS • TOKYO • MILAN
MADRID • WARSAW • BUDAPEST • AUCKLAND

Original hardcover edition published in 1992
by Mills & Boon Limited

ISBN 0-373-03234-X

Harlequin Romance first edition November 1992

SUMMER'S ECHO

CHAPTER ONE

As THE plane began its steady descent towards Bordeaux's Mérignac Airport Roxanne saw Jeannie's knuckles tighten on the arms of her seat. Her lips moved, as though she were muttering to herself, but no sound issued from them.

'What are you doing?' Roxanne asked curiously.

'I'm praying,' came the freelance photographer's rather grim reply.

Roxanne turned her head to look out of the window, a faint smile lighting her features. Although she had worked with Jeannie many times, they had not travelled abroad together before today, but the other girl had the reputation of being a nervous flier.

As for Roxanne herself, her mouth was dry and her stomach knotted as the plane came down over the long triangular spit of the Médoc, with the blue line of the Atlantic ruled straight along one side, and the broad Gironde estuary ribbon-like along the other, but her nervous distress had nothing to do with a dislike of being airborne.

It would be truer to say that her problems would only be beginning when the plane taxied to a halt. Yet in a sense their roots stretched back over five long years.

I never thought I would ever come back here again, she mused to herself. Left to her own devices, she most probably never would have. Why was fate so fiendish and capricious as to hand her just what she wanted, in the last place on earth she would have chosen to seek for it?

She concentrated on the fast-approaching city straddling the silver confluence of the Dordogne and Garonne Rivers, its roof-tops, squares and parks becoming clearer by the second, and it was as if she caught a whiff of the salty, tangy air blowing in freshly over the wide quays. Imagination, of course, but she took a deep, instinctive breath in order to savour it. There was no doubt that Bordeaux was a splendid city, however unhappy the memories it held for her.

'Look, Jeannie,' she tried to allay her companion's fears, 'we're almost there! We'll be landing any minute. Look how magnificent it is!'

Jeannie opened her tightly closed eyes for long enough to peer quickly out.

'Huh! Maybe, but I'll appreciate it better when the wheels touch the ground!' she snorted. Then her curiosity briefly got the better of her apprehension. 'You've been here before, haven't you?' she asked.

Roxanne leaned back in her seat and forced herself to speak casually.

'Oh, it was some time ago,' she said. 'But you won't need to rely on me to direct us. Didier Joly, the *négociant's* representative, will be here at the airport to meet us.'

The aircraft touched down smoothly, and Roxanne felt the tension flowing out of the other girl as she realised that solid ground was once more beneath her. Simultaneously her own disquiet began to increase dangerously, and she swallowed hard. She was back in this city, Alain's city, and she did not need Monsieur Joly or anyone else to help her find her way around. For, even though Alain, mercifully, was three thousand miles away across the Atlantic, her feet would rediscover of their own accord the streets she had once trodden hand in hand with him.

She took a firm, determined grip on her wayward emotions. Nostalgia was a pathetic, self-indulgent luxury she could not afford. No one at Courtney and Weaver knew anything about that unfortunate period of her life before she'd joined them, more than four years earlier, as a public relations assistant. It had been over and buried, then; she certainly was not about to resurrect it, now.

She and Jeannie had left London a few hours ago on a temperamentally English summer day of coy sunshine and squally showers. Here the sun was warm and bright in a high, spacious blue sky, the tarmac was hot under their feet, with a lingering late-afternoon warmth which declared itself only a respite from fiercer midday temperatures. Summer in the Médoc was a different animal, and Roxanne could not repress a brief, reminiscent tremor.

Customs formalities over, luggage collected, they looked around them for signs of anyone who might have the air of having been delegated to meet two strange females. They did not know Didier Joly, nor he them.

'Miss Jefferson is...let's see, about five feet seven, that's one metre seventy to you, Didier, with longish fair hair and green eyes, and a no-nonsense manner...you could describe her as a sort of super-efficient naiad,' her boss had said over the telephone as he'd finalised the arrangements, eyes gleaming wickedly as Roxanne had pulled disgusted faces at him across his desk. 'Miss Nutley resembles an outraged midget wearing a red feather-duster on her head. They should be instantly identifiable.'

Jeannie shook her same scarlet curls worriedly now as she gazed up at Roxanne.

'D'you reckon they've forgotten about us?' she demanded.

'Oh, surely not,' Roxanne reassured her briskly. 'But not to worry. If no one shows up we'll take a taxi to our hotel, and I'll personally phone and give Monsieur Joly a rocket!'

Being back in Bordeaux was getting to her already, before they had even left the airport, and she felt she might welcome the chance to vent her nervous reactions on someone. Really, it was too bad!

'It doesn't augur too well for the smooth running of the campaign, though,' she said irritably. 'I shall have something to say about this.'

'I shouldn't complain too loudly if I were you,' a dry, quiet voice with an undertone of dark humour spoke up from just behind her left shoulder in excellent, faintly accented English. 'It isn't poor Didier's fault. Unfortunately he sprained his wrist in a riding accident yesterday evening, and is in some pain. He sent me in his place, along with his sincere regrets.'

For a split-second Roxanne was paralysed. This could not be happening! It was impossible that he was here at all, when she had presumed him safely in America; therefore this must be a nightmare from which she would soon awake to a less dangerous reality. But she knew that voice beyond any uncertainty. It had spoken to her softly and caressingly in the night. It had torn her to shreds with its icy, logical scorn.

She turned around, unwillingly, and there he was. Alain Deslandes, slim, grave and elegant in dark couture trousers and a white shirt, tie-less, with his jacket hooked over his shoulder by one finger, his other hand already being clasped by Jeannie, who was effusive with relief that they had been met after all. Unruffled by the heat, a few more flecks of grey in his dark brown hair, perhaps an extra line or two engraved in the high, intelligent brow.

Recognition, but no surprise, and no real welcome in the dark grey blue-flecked eyes.

'Roxanne.'

'*Alain!*'

He spoke quietly, measuring her from a distance. He was obviously prepared for this encounter, and either had no strong feelings about it, or else had schooled himself so to appear—with Alain it had always been difficult to tell. He could erect an impenetrable barrier of calm detachment, seemingly at will, and it was wrapped around him now.

She, on the other hand, was totally surprised and reeling from the shock. It was impossible for her to keep this from becoming evident. He had her at a disadvantage. But then, hadn't he always?

'What are you doing here?' she gasped almost accusingly. 'You're supposed to be in the States!'

'Really?' His eyebrows lifted slightly with amused disdain. 'I don't know who supposed that to be the case, other than yourself.'

Jeannie stared fascinatedly from one to the other as she picked up the vibrations that hummed in the air.

'You two know each other?' she asked unnecessarily.

'We're acquainted,' he replied laconically with what Roxanne resentfully thought was deliberately slighting ambiguity. *Acquainted?* The passionate summer of their love, the ensuing heartbreak, the bitter acrimony of their parting? How typical of him to belittle all that—and her—in one short but carefully chosen phrase.

Jeannie was looking nonplussed and uncertain how to deal with the current flowing between this urbanely elegant Frenchman and her stony-faced colleague. Alain smiled at her, and Roxanne saw, sickeningly, that the effect on the photographer was immediate. Alain's smile was like that. It relaxed his face from stern authority to a youthful charm, shedding him of ten years in an instant.

'Alain Deslandes,' he introduced himself. 'And you are Jeannie Nutley? I'm familiar with your work.'

Jeannie's delighted grin split her face beneath its outrageous mop of red hair. 'You are?' she squealed, and Roxanne was hard put not to snort with annoyance. Jeannie was an up-and-coming photographer who had a good deal of successful assignments under her belt. There was no need for her to behave like a schoolgirl who had just had her first photos printed in the Guides' magazine!

She gave her colleague a nudge.

'Jeannie...what about your equipment?' she muttered pointedly. Instead of fussing about her cameras, meters and lenses, as she usually did when out on a job, Jeannie was engrossed in gazing raptly at Alain.

She snapped back to earth guiltily.

'Oh, lord, yes! Monsieur Deslandes...our personal luggage is all here, but they seem to have mislaid my equipment.'

'Leave it to me. I'll see to it,' he said with reassuring briskness, and Roxanne was quite sure that he would. Alain was so damn capable, so infuriatingly competent; was there anything with which he could not cope?

The two women watched his swift but unhurried progress across the concourse, and Jeannie looked at Roxanne with a thousand questions in her sharp blue eyes. However, she restricted herself to the only one which seemed appropriate right at that moment.

'What an incredible dish of a feller! Did you know him well?'

Roxanne sighed. In view of the fact that Alain was here, it was useless for her to embark on a pretence about their past relationship. There was certainly no reason to believe that *he* would feel obliged to do so, so she might as well tell the truth.

'I thought I did,' she said bluntly, trying to keep the note of wistful sadness from creeping, unwanted, into her voice. 'I lived here with him once. He was my husband.'

Roxanne had not been directly involved with the Bien Vivre Wine campaign from its inception. For one thing, it was a very large account, which had always been handled by Roland Weaver, one of Courtney and Weaver's directors. Roland had known Bien Vivre's English managing director personally, and had taken on their publicity years earlier, back in the days when the wine importers were a struggling new concern, and he and Toby Courtney had just set up their public relations consultancy.

But Roland had recently taken early retirement, owing to ill-health, and Toby, in his wisdom, had decreed that the new, upmarket line of fine wines Bien Vivre was about to launch had need of some equally new young blood to steer it into the market-place. Toby now saw himself as the captain of the ship, deciding overall policy and delegating authority, rather than involving himself with individual clients, and, with audacious faith in his youngest lieutenant, he'd allocated Bien Vivre to Roxanne.

Tempting as the prospect was from a career point of view, Roxanne had at first argued against his decision, protesting that she was too young, too inexperienced, that the account was too big and too important to the consultancy. How could he take such a risk?

Toby had leaned back in his capacious chair—it had to be capacious, because Toby weighed fifteen stone—and lit yet another of his endless cigars.

'I wonder why you are playing devil's advocate, my girl?' he had mused speculatively. 'For the past year you've been badgering me to give you greater responsibilities. You weren't fully stretched, you said—as if you were a nylon stocking, for goodness' sake! Now here I am, handing you a plum account, and you turn tail and pull the helpless-female trick on me! Whatever happened to all that determined feminism?'

Roxanne was beached high and dry by his argument. But she fought on for a while.

'This has nothing to do with gender, Toby. You could say I'm just plain scared that this one will be too much for me.'

'Of course you are. You'll be running scared the whole time until the campaign is launched, and then you'll be even more scared, waiting for the results,' he pronounced practically. 'It's that same fear which will spur you on, and pump the adrenalin that fires the creative engine. Public relations is no place for shrinking violets who want to play safe. Now open the window, for goodness' sake—this office is like a saloon bar, minus the beer.'

Roxanne forbore to point out that it was his interminable cigar smoke which rendered the atmosphere stale and perpetually hazy. Deep down she knew she refused this assignment at her peril. She was washed up at Courtney and Weaver, and probably in the entire public-relations world, if she did so. Nor were her chances any too rosy if she was identified with a campaign which failed. Not only did she have to do it, but she had to do it well.

'It looks like heads you win, tails I lose,' she stated philosophically, forcing up the window sash to admit a little fresh air into the office. When she turned back Toby was contentedly puffing out more blue clouds to combat the input.

'That's a fair assessment of the situation,' he agreed, adding reasonably, 'There's very little point in my employing an account executive who speaks fluent French if I can't make full use of her talents when the occasion arises. You are uniquely qualified for this job, Roxanne.'

She checked herself on the point of warning him that her 'fluent' French was somewhat out of practice, and that she had not so much as set foot on French soil in four years. It had already been decided that the job was hers. Why make waves by protesting further?

All her stated objections had been perfectly valid. Bien Vivre *was* a large account, more prestigious than anything she had hitherto been allowed to handle, and the prospect was exhilaratingly frightening. Her career rested on how she performed now, and on the results of this campaign depended her progress from relatively untried junior account executive all the way up the ladder—as far as directorship, or even the possibility of opening her own consultancy at some time in the future, if she wanted to go that far.

But, although it was true to say that any launch of a new line for a valued client would have scared and elated her, she could not deny that this was subtly different. What filled her with apprehension now was the journey back into her own past, to a time and place, a series of events she had fought hard to forget, and to put behind her.

She could not have explained all that to Toby. When she'd joined Courtney and Weaver all she had divulged about her personal life was that she was recently divorced, and unattached. The ending of her brief marriage had been so traumatic and painful that she had quite literally been unable to talk about it. Nor had she wished to. She had hoped that if she did not refer to it maybe she would stop thinking about it, and if she stopped thinking about it perhaps soon she could pretend that it had never happened. It was a closed book she went through life refusing to open, even to take a peep. Until now.

Until now, when she found herself sitting in the front seat of Alain's car as he drove away from the airport, and even that had not been of her choosing. The luggage had gone in the boot, Jeannie's equipment had been stacked on the back seat, and Jeannie had clambered in protectively with it, leaving only one place vacant for Roxanne.

Certainly she had not wanted to be that close to her ex-husband, aware of his clean, spare profile as he looked straight ahead at the traffic, trying not to watch his long, capable hands lying easily atop the steering-wheel. Hands she had once loved to kiss, that had touched her face tenderly and driven her body wild. She most definitely did not want to think of *that*.

'I take it you have not visited Bordeaux before, Miss Nutley?' he enquired politely in English, having obviously realised quickly that Jeannie's command of French was so slight as to be non-existent.

'Please call me Jeannie—everyone does. No, Bordeaux is quite new to me, but it looks very interesting,' she bubbled. 'I'm certainly looking forward to getting out and about with my camera.'

'You'll find plenty of subject matter. There is a medieval quarter with many fine fifteenth and sixteenth century buildings, but much of the commercial and administrative centre was laid out in the eighteenth century, when the wine trade really began to prosper. And, of course, there are the quays and docks. Bordeaux's trade was born along its riverfront.'

He turned the car easily into the busy flow of traffic along the broad Allée de Tourny, flanked by many imposing buildings erected over a century earlier, exuding wealth, stability, and a breadth of urbane culture.

'But, of course, you have Roxanne, who knows her way around only too well, and will be an excellent guide,' he murmured.

Murder in her heart, she shot him an oblique glance which only partly concealed her growing hostility. She had not been deaf to the faint unpleasantness lurking in his last remark, which had seemed, on the surface, innocent enough. Alain was a master of that kind of subtly crushing double meaning when he chose to be.

'I doubt I could remember my bearings without a map after so long,' she said with attempted nonchalance, burning to make it plain that he and his city were part of a past she had all but forgotten. 'You would do better by far with Alain as a guide, Jeannie. He's a history lecturer, and could doubtless explain the significance of every archway and gable.'

Alain was not at all perturbed by this. He grinned—that disturbing smile which transformed him from aloof authoritarian to Boy Scout—and Roxanne's stomach performed a plummeting dive worthy of a lift in a hundred-storey skyscraper.

'If I am ever short of gainful employment I can always apply to you for a reference in order to earn a living as a tour guide,' he remarked cheerfully. 'Here we are, ladies, on the Cours de l'Intendance. Many of these superb mansions you see now were built as dwelling houses for wealthy merchants and personalities of note, viz. the Hotel Acquart, which we are just passing. How am I doing?'

Jeannie giggled appreciatively, and Roxanne held down—just—a sigh of exasperation. Alain could be wryly funny like this while, underneath the humour, a sinister intelligence was hard at work. She was uncomfortably sure that he was no more pleased to see her than she was to see him, but it had been obvious, even at the airport, that he had known whose arrival he was awaiting. He had had a choice, and, knowing that the encounter could hold no pleasure for him, he had elected to come. Why?

They turned into the Esplanade des Quinconces to a breathtaking view of the lofty pillar of the Girondin Monument crowned by its triumphant winged figure. Prancing bronze horses surrounded its base, and playing fountains spouted jets of crystal water, the whole flanked by an imposing square of vast proportions.

'You are missing your cue,' Roxanne could not resist sniping at him. 'Here you should tell us that the Place des Quinconces is the largest square in Europe. I'm afraid I should not wish to employ you.'

'I am upstaged,' he commented philosophically.

Roxanne doubted he was ever that, but she was full of questions as to why he was here at all, and finally she could no longer suppress her urgent need for answers.

'What puzzles me is how you come to be standing in for Didier Joly,' she said a little snappily. 'As I said earlier, the last I heard you were lecturing at a university in America.'

It was hard to keep the note of accusation out of her voice, almost as if she was telling him he had no right to be here in this, the city of his birth when she had imagined him safely the other side of the ocean.

The look he bestowed on her, considering, slightly contemptuous, made it clear he was aware of her annoyance, and unconcerned by it.

'The world is very small these days, Roxanne,' he said calmly. 'As a matter of fact, since you insist on knowing what is really none of your business, I returned very re-

cently on a year's sabbatical. I'm working on a book
about the history of the region. Does that satisfy you?'

'Oh, really, Alain, I could not care less why you are
here—or, at least, only in so far as it *does* concern me,'
she retorted testily. 'I'm here to do a job of work, and
expected to be met by someone who knows a little about
it.'

He shrugged dismissively. 'And obviously you have
scant sympathy for poor Didier, who is stuffed full of
pain-killers and in no condition to drive at the moment,'
he said in a voice full of reproof. 'There's really no great
mystery about my presence. I've known Didier for years,
and he rang me at short notice and asked me to pick up
a Miss Roxanne Jefferson and Miss Jean Nutley from
the airport. Should I have refused to do a friend this
small favour?'

Roxanne had not meant to sound unsympathetic, but
somehow Alain had trapped her neatly into making much
ado about very little.

'Of course, I'm sorry that Monsieur Joly is hurt,' she
said. 'I quite understand the situation. But we have a
tight schedule, with several appointments and visits set
up, for which he is our contacts man. Driving is not a
problem—I can always drive myself. But will he be well
enough to accompany us?'

Alain was busy guiding the vehicle down a narrow
street on the fringe of old Bordeaux, and at first he did
not answer her question.

'Here's your hotel,' he said. 'I expect you will want
to settle in and have an early night, and I'm sure you
will be comfortable here. However, should you feel like
a stroll you are only minutes from the Rue Ste-Catherine
and the heart of the old quarter. In case you had forgotten, that is.'

Roxanne looked up sharply at that last dig, and caught him watching her very carefully, his eyes very sharp and alert in a closed, thoughtful face. She remembered with sudden, piercing clarity their evening walks along the Rue Ste-Catherine during their brief courtship. The summer throngs spilling out over the pavement cafés. His arm around her shoulders. His voice in her ear, wry and amusing.

Wanting him. Wanting to go somewhere alone with him, to lie in his arms and make love, but afraid of the immensity of her own need, of the deep significance of the unknown experience he represented. She wondered if he, too, was remembering that romantic, inexperienced girl, and a shameful colour crept up her neck, stinging the pallor of her cheeks with a betraying pink flush.

But I loved you so much then, she thought sadly. Didn't you know, don't you know still? I truly did. I couldn't handle it. It was all too fierce, too overwhelming, too entirely unexpected.

Too late, now, for explanations.

'Thank you, yes,' she said in a clipped voice. 'I think I can find my way that far.'

A porter came out from the hotel to take their luggage, and Roxanne thought gratefully, At last I can get away from him, away from this awful situation which I hate, and which he, in some perverse, awful way, seems almost to be relishing.

'And thank you for collecting us from the airport,' she said formally. 'It was very kind of you. I expect that Didier Joly will be in touch?'

Alain's smile was no more than a cold shadow flitting across his lean academic's face.

'Not for a day or two he won't,' he told her. 'Perhaps I did not explain fully. Didier is *hors de combat*. For the moment, I am afraid, you will have to put up with me.'

As he bent to retrieve Jeannie's cameras from the back seat his face was briefly close to Roxanne's, so that only she heard him add with dry resignation, 'And vice versa.'

The hotel was cool and comfortable, and Roxanne and Jeannie each had a large, airy room to themselves, so Roxanne was able to escape on the pretext of unpacking, and avoid an immediate barrage of questions.

But she knew this could only be a postponement, and could not honestly blame Jeannie for being curious about this unexpected turn of events. She had, after all, been an innocent bystander who could not avoid being affected by the verbal skirmishing which had started up between Alain and herself from the moment they had first set eyes on each other again at the airport.

No one connected with Roxanne had been aware that her ex-husband was French, and that this working trip was a return to the part of the world where she had once lived with him. The reserve, the fear of disturbing memories of the past which had kept her quiet for so long, must have appeared as deliberate secrecy. But she really had nothing to hide from others—only things from which she herself was still in hiding.

Although only a stone's throw from the city's modern quarter, and equally close to its medieval heart, the hotel had a courtyard patio which was an oasis of quiet, and here the two young women met for a drink before dinner. The heat had faded now, but the old walls still trapped the warmth, and the sky was a pale azure, glimpsed through a tracery of trees, and just beginning to darken.

Roxanne sipped a *pastis* reflectively, and Jeannie drank Bacardi laced with Coke.

'I don't know how you can stomach that aniseed stuff—it tastes like dentists' mouthwash,' she grinned. 'I suppose it's a habit you picked up when you lived here?'

It was as good an opener as any, Roxanne conceded.

'I suppose so. Another I picked up was arguing with Alain, and old habits die hard,' she said. 'I'm sorry if we caused you any embarrassment. Hopefully Didier Joly will soon be back in business, and we shan't be obliged to spend any more time in my ex's company.'

'I wasn't embarrassed, merely curious, and I don't mind his company in the least. I find him quite charming. In fact, if I weren't "spoken for"...' Jeannie looked enquiringly at Roxanne over the rim of her glass. 'However did you let *that* one get away? You must be crazy.'

Roxanne could not repress a smile.

'And you're incorrigible. Does that Gary of yours know how much time you spend talent-spotting?'

'He knows I only look, and don't maul the goods,' Jeannie laughed. 'Seriously, though—what happened? You two can't have been married for very long.'

Roxanne steepled her fingers and rested her chin on them.

'Only for about a year,' she said quietly. 'It was so obviously a mistake that we decided to cut our losses. What happened was that I was too young, and went in too deep, too quickly. It all went badly wrong. There isn't a lot more I can say about it, and it's not a period of my life I enjoy remembering, or talking about, Jeannie, so can we leave it at that?'

Jeannie took one look at the other girl's closed expression, which was echoed by her tight, controlled voice, and realised that she was in deadly earnest. This was not an area for exploration.

'Point taken,' she agreed quickly. 'But, one way or another, it looks as if you are going to be seeing a fair amount of Alain over the next few days. Can you cope with that? The vibes in the car on the drive from the airport were humming so much that they almost knocked me over.'

'Well, you must realise it was something of a shock, meeting him again like that so unexpectedly,' Roxanne excused herself. 'But we are both adults, and it was all over between us a long time ago.'

'All?' Jeannie repeated, swirling the ice thoughtfully in the bottom of her glass. 'Are you sure? You certainly seemed to have the wind taken out of your sails.'

'I am quite, quite sure,' Roxanne said emphatically. 'It's a closed chapter. I've made another life for myself now, and so has Alain, without any doubt. Obviously I loved him once, or believed I did. But we're both different people now.'

She smiled, indicating that the subject was firmly closed, and picked up the menu.

'*Hungry* people, incidentally. Shall we order now, or would you like another drink first?'

'Let's eat. And, OK, I know a red light when I see one,' Jeannie capitulated. 'But there's one thing I haven't quite grasped. Didier Joly is a *négociant*, right? His business is buying and selling wine. Alain is a lecturer in history. Is he qualified to take Didier's place, even temporarily? I mean, he seems frightfully knowledgeable about Bordeaux, but still...'

'I shouldn't worry on that score.' Roxanne's voice was wry. 'Alain may not be in the wine trade, but here in Bordeaux it's in the blood. He's the son and grandson of *négociants*, and knows everyone who is anyone in the business. And what he doesn't know about Bordeaux, the Médoc, and the entire area wouldn't cover the back of a wine label!'

'It sounds as if we'll be in capable hands,' Jeannie said thoughtfully.

'Without the shadow of a doubt.' There was just a hint of resentment lurking behind Roxanne's categorical reply. 'What Alain sets out to do he accomplishes thoroughly and with flair. I might add that he will expect the same of us, so we had best keep our wits about us. There's another side to that charm you were so knocked out by.'

All that she had said was true, she reflected as they went in to dinner. All of it? Well...the greater part. Alain was an internationally acknowledged expert on the region and its history. He was also a perfectionist who could be scathing with those who did not give of their best and failed to live up to his high standards.

But something she had told Jeannie earlier nagged at the back of her mind and would give her no peace.

We're both different people now, she had said. But were they? Alain had been thirty when she'd first met him, already successful in his academic career, already a mature man, whose opinions, ideals and behaviour had been forged in the furnace of experience. He had been confident, impatient, sure of what he thought and what he wanted.

On the evidence of their admittedly short reacquaintance, he did not appear to have changed. He was still the same Alain she remembered, who had overturned her life and broken her trusting young heart.

And she herself? On the surface she was very different. She knew she gave the impression of a successful young career woman, in command of herself and sure of where she was going. Cool, polished, friendly, if a little reserved, there would seem to be nothing left of the naïve, passionate, confused girl who had fallen in love so helplessly five years earlier.

Only Roxanne could not wholly suppress the suspicion that she had not completely killed off her former self—that, buried beneath the composed façade, she still lurked, bruised and trembling.

More than that, she was terribly afraid that Alain Deslandes still had the power to crack that smooth surface, exposing to the merciless light of day the frightened creature in hiding there.

Let it not be too long, she prayed, the time in which she had to endure his presence, his calm wit, his thoughtful, mocking stare... and yes, his undeniable physical appeal that still rocked her, reluctant as she was to admit it. Let it not be long, and *please*, she added desperately, give me the strength to survive!

CHAPTER TWO

ROXANNE heard every church bell in the old city chime two before sleep claimed her, and as she had requested a seven o'clock morning call she did not awake feeling bright and refreshed.

Pull yourself together, girl, she exhorted herself sternly, splashing her face with cold water and then rubbing it briskly with a towel. She peered critically at her reflection, hoping she did not look bleary-eyed.

What had Toby jokingly called her—a super-efficient naiad? The oval face with its small, straight nose and neat little chin, which dimpled slightly when she smiled, had always made her look younger than her years, and still did. Perhaps when she was forty she would be grateful for it. As it was, she tended to compensate by wearing a cool, detached expression when she wanted to be taken seriously, tightening her lips to refine their natural generosity.

Since she never really studied herself when her face was relaxed—a feat virtually impossible for anyone—she wasn't fully aware of the power of her smile; if she had been she might have realised that it accomplished far more for her than any amount of efficient severity. Her sweet smile, together with the buoyant swing of her straight mid-length blonde hair, the colour of wheat streaked with silver, and the astonishing clarity of her unusual green eyes, were a head-turning combination.

Today it was somehow vitally important to her that she looked her best. A rumpled, untidy public-relations person was a contradiction in terms in her opinion, since

she did not see how one could come across as a con-
vincing image-maker and be less than personally impec-
cable. She was always crisp and groomed and well
turned-out, and had schooled herself to pay particular
attention to the little details which counted for so much—
smooth unsnagged tights, well-heeled shoes which were
kept polished, and a good, perfectly shaped haircut
which did not lose its style every time a puff of wind
disturbed it.

But even as she zipped up the skirt of her cool, well-
tailored, linen-look beige suit she did not fool herself
that professional pride was the only force at work today.
The suit was ideal; it had an inverted-pleat skirt which
would not impede her movements, and a long-line
jacket—correct, businesslike and fashionable at the same
time. Roxanne frowned as she slipped on shoes which
were not only smart, but comfortable to walk in, for
today they were to visit the *négociant's chai*, where the
wine was stored, racked and blended. Should she be
wondering, at the same time, how she would look to
Alain's eyes, and what impression she would make on
the man to whom she had once been married, who had
rocketed back so unexpectedly into her life?

Why should I care? she thought resentfully. What did
it matter if he thought her looks had deteriorated, if he
found her less appealing than the girl he had successfully wooed five years earlier?

Still, she was only human, and honest enough to admit
that it *did* matter, if only to drive home the message that
she was fine, doing very nicely, thank you, and that un-
loading him had been the wisest day's work she had ever
done! So the short-sleeved blouse she put on under her
jacket for when the day grew hotter was of a striking
orange and brown jungle print, and she wore swinging
gold and coral earrings and a matching bracelet.

'Nice touch,' Jeannie said approvingly as they met for breakfast. She was too good at her profession not to notice form, composition and effect. 'It isn't easy, I suppose, in your line of business, to choose the right clothes. After all, you have to make two very different statements about yourself at the same time. One, I am a competent, reliable businesswoman, and two, I am a live-wire creative thinker. Not simple.'

Roxanne grinned over her coffee and *chocolate de pain*. Her companion was wearing brilliant pink trousers and top, her equally bright hair tied back with a pink and turquoise silk bandanna.

'Whereas you, lucky girl, can get away with saying "I'm wacky and original". Right?' she riposted.

'Right. I don't have to impress my ex-husband, either. I'll have to be content just to catch Alain's eye, because I guess I'm not really his type, and Gary would kill me if I tried anything more.'

Roxanne's smile faded promptly.

'Forget it, Jeannie. I am not out to impress Alain,' she insisted, and as the other girl's eyebrows rose sceptically she had the grace to qualify her statement. 'Well, at least, not in the way that you mean.'

'There's another way?' Jeannie bit into her croissant with gusto.

'Of course there is.' Roxanne was frowning again, knew it, and made a conscious effort to stop. It made one appear bad-tempered and difficult. 'The only thing I want to impress upon Alain is that my life is much better without him.'

'Um.' Jeannie chewed vigorously. 'Quite sure you've convinced yourself of that, are you?'

Roxanne folded up her napkin, her quick, jerky movements betraying a faint anger.

'I'm positive. I've got an interesting career which I love, and excellent prospects; my own flat; friends whose company I enjoy. And, if I feel the need for male companionship, there's Stuart,' she added, almost as an afterthought.

Jeannie laughed.

'Oh, yes. Don't forget the ever-persistent Stuart. One of these days he'll get fed up with waiting to see which way you decide to jump,' she warned darkly.

'It isn't like that. We're just friends,' Roxanne protested. 'I value that friendship, whatever you might say, Jeannie.'

The other girl still looked dubious.

'I'm willing to bet you and Alain weren't ''friends'',' she said knowingly.

Roxanne looked down into the milky, swirling surface of her *café au lait*, and her face clouded over.

'No,' she said softly, 'we weren't.'

To be strictly fair, it had to be said that there had hardly been time for anything as considered and time-consuming as friendship to develop between them. One moment he had been a stranger to her, and the next she had been wildly and extravagantly in love. It had all happened so quickly, between one heartbeat and the next. Across a crowded room. A bolt from the blue. Swept off her feet. All the silly, hackneyed old clichés had all come true for her... as surely as they must do often enough for them to *become* clichés in the first place. But she had not realised that at the time. She had thought she was unique—chosen, deeply, deeply privileged, and at the same time fatefully doomed.

Although just turned twenty then, she knew now that she had been young for her years. She had grown up in the industrial northern town of Sheffield, where she had been a bright schoolgirl who excelled at English and foreign languages. Her mother had died suddenly, just as Roxanne had been taking her A Levels and deciding on her educational future. Always close to her father, she had been drawn even closer to him by the mutual bereavement, and reluctance to leave him alone at this crisis point in his life had been one of the factors which had made her decide to study at the local polytechnic. The other was that it ran a business studies course combined with languages, which was highly regarded and tailor-made for her talents.

Roxanne enjoyed the course, and her college years, but she was never the typical student. While her fellow students lived in halls of residence where, in their spare time, they threw noisy parties and fell in and out of love with one another, she went home every evening and weekend to the neat semi-detached house in Hillsborough which had been her childhood home. She had plenty of friends, and was well-liked, but always at one remove from the pulsating interior life of the college. Thus she avoided many of the mistakes her peers made—there were no injudicious affairs or experimental relationships—but mistakes were the building blocks of learning how to live, and Roxanne was not equipped with this educational armour.

The summer in France, arranged by her tutor, was supposed to perfect her French and broaden her experience, and in the event it did both, more thoroughly than could have been expected.

The city of Bordeaux caught her breath and her imagination from the very first day of her stay here. It enchanted her, and yet she felt oddly at home. There was culture and beauty aplenty to appreciate, but Roxanne instinctively felt the pulse of a city which existed primarily through trade—after all, she came from another, and, even though the trades were different, the mores, the outlook, were not dissimilar. 'I produce and sell, therefore I am' was the statement which quivered in the air along the wide boulevards and in the cathedral-like temples of wine.

Roxanne worked in the Office de Tourisme. Since she did not know the city well, as did the trained and experienced regular staff, and her French was still a little hesitant, she could not call herself anything more than a 'dogsbody'. But it was interesting, she learned quickly, and her command of the language improved rapidly with every day that passed.

She had a room at a student hostel, and made superficial friendships with the few mostly foreign students who were obliged to remain there for the summer, but her chief pleasure and entertainment in her free time was walking the streets of the city, guide book in hand, learning her way about it. Not only did this help her in her work at the tourist office, but it gave her a growing love for and a sense of belonging to Bordeaux and the Bordelais, whom she found reserved, in a way an English person instinctively understood, but invariably friendly and helpful.

'Enough of this endless pavement-pounding,' a senior colleague said to her, kindly but sternly, one Friday morning in mid-July. 'It's time you had some social life. How else will you get to know anyone here?'

'There are other students at the hostel,' Roxanne protested with a shy smile.

'Who are all very nice, I'm sure, but are probably Thais and Nigerians. You should meet the French on their home ground. My wife and I are going to a cocktail party tonight, at the home of a respected *négociant. Le tout Bordeaux* will be there. Why not come along?'

Roxanne demurred politely, but he was insistent, and finally she was obliged to give in. Part of her reluctance

was a fear of not having the right thing to wear for such
an occasion. Bordeaux was full of smart shops and
boutiques displaying lovely clothes, but not at prices her
student budget could afford, so she wore what she called
her 'boring black' which she saved for lecturers' at-home
parties and the like, and had only thrown into her suitcase
on a last-minute impulse.

Compared to the elegant outfits worn by the women
in the spacious drawing-room of the big old merchant's
house on the Rue du Quai, not far from the quays, as
its name suggested, it was a very cheap dress. But at
least it was simple and uncluttered. And, although she
did not realise it, the plain straight skirt and scoop-neck
bodice, combined with her slender, leggy youthfulness
and the long blonde hair caught at the nape of her neck
with a black velvet bow, made her a vision of appealing
beauty many of the more expensively clad older women
might have envied.

Roxanne stood quietly sipping her glass of excellent
Graves, smiling and speaking when spoken to. The home
of *négociant* Frederic Deslandes and his wife Mathilde
was faintly intimidating to the girl from a middle-class
background. There was old money here—venerable
Turkey and Bokhara carpets, parquet with a silken patina
of age, fine paintings and antique furniture, none of
which looked like reproductions.

All around her rose and fell the buzz of swift, cultured French voices as the commercial aristocracy and
the intelligentsia met and mingled. They talked art,
politics, business—and occasionally, as at all gath-
erings, voices dropped to a whisper, and Roxanne assumed they must be talking about each other!

And then, without knowing quite how it happened,
she became separated from the kindly couple who had

brought her along, and she found herself adrift in this sophisticated crowd, without an anchor.

She looked around her anxiously, feeling conspicuous in her solitary state; the only person not involved in rapt conversation, she thought she must stand out like a sore thumb, although, at the same time, it seemed that no one was taking any notice of her.

And then it occurred to her that someone was. Over the heads of several groups, and clear across the other side of the room, a man was looking at her, his expression thoughtful, questioning, with just a hint of humour. He was a little over average height, with an aura of quietly composed self-possession, and an utter confidence so complete that it did not need to be flaunted. Straight, thick, well-cut dark brown hair emphasised the spare lines of a lean, clever face which looked as if it knew all the answers. A level gaze which missed little held hers, linking her to him by an unseen, intangible thread, ignoring the intervening space and the hum of chatter as though they did not exist.

He smiled. A sudden lightening of his features gave him a boyish, almost mischievous air quite at odds with the rest of his appearance. A shock of something that could only be called recognition hit Roxanne full and hard in the solar plexus, rendering her quite literally breathless.

She knew this man. He had been waiting for her, as she had been waiting for this moment throughout aeons of time and light years of endless space.

It was he who moved, crossing the room, making his way through the throng towards her, but nevertheless it felt to Roxanne as though he were reeling in the thread, drawing her out of the safe camouflage in which she swam, swinging her high in the air like a landed, floundering fish. Dizziness assailed her, and for a moment she panicked. Then he was at her side, and it was all right, it was how it had to be.

'One very rarely sees a new face at these occasions,' he said, his voice calm, quite deep, and full of a reserve of reflective wit. 'We have not been introduced, but then I've only just arrived. Alain Deslandes.'

He put out his hand, and obediently, still in a mild daze, she put hers into it. His grip was firm and cool, but too brief, and when he released her fingers she felt strangely forlorn.

'I'm very happy to make your acquaintance,' she managed to reply faintly. Deslandes? Wasn't that the name of her hosts? she thought, mustering her intelligence through a haze of confusion.

Again the smile, a little knowing this time.

'Ah. English.' He switched painlessly from one language to the other, and Roxanne was still too bedazzled by the odd emotion which had seized her to care that her accent had betrayed her origins. 'But you are not a student at the university, or I would have seen you before.'

'Roxanne Jefferson,' she finally found the strength to introduce herself. 'I've just finished a course at Sheffield Polytechnic, and I'm working here at the Office de Tourisme for the summer.'

The words came out automatically, but it did not really matter what she said, so long as it kept him at her side, so long as he did not drift off, out of her sphere, where she could lay no claim on his attention. His eyes rested on her now, and she observed minutely the flecks of blue in the deep grey irises as if her very life depended on her being able to recall their exact hue tomorrow.

'Ah. Then I presume you must have come along with Georges and Sophie.'

Through a gap in the shifting groups of people
Roxanne saw her colleague's wife looking around the
room, anxiously searching for her young charge. Then
she caught sight of Roxanne talking to Alain Deslandes,
and flashed her a quick smile of approval before turning
back to the friend to whom she had been chatting.

Roxanne's relief was overwhelming. She did not want
to be rescued. She did not want to be torn away from
this man. But for how long could she hold him? Perhaps
he had only taken pity on her because she had looked
lonely and out of place. Perhaps he had a partner somewhere in the room . . . wife . . . girlfriend . . . No, her inner
self screamed in outrage, he can't have, he must *not*
belong to someone else! What in heaven's name was
happening to her? They had only just *met*!

'Yes, that's right. I'm so glad I did—this is such a
beautiful house. It must be very old,' she heard herself
babbling. Anything to keep the conversation going!
'Monsieur and Madame Deslandes, they are . . .'

'My parents,' he supplied. 'You have almost as in-
triguing an accent in English as you do in French. Are
you Scottish? No, I don't think that's it. And I once
spent some time in Newcastle, so I know you are not a
Geordie.'

'It's Yorkshire. Sheffield is my home town,' she informed him. 'Actually I didn't think I had much of an
accent.'

'A trace. But don't try to lose it—it's charming and
individual,' he told her. 'We Bordelais have one too, of
course. There are those who claim it owes something to
the influx of English settlers here over the centuries. I
think that's a trifle fanciful, but it's a fact that the
Bordeaux telephone directory has a fair sprinkling of
English-sounding names.'

'Is that true?' She looked up into his eyes, genuine interest surfacing through the swirling smog of emotions she could not explain or justify.

'Well, yes. Aquitaine was once an English province, as I expect you know. Eleanor of Aquitaine brought it under the English crown as her dowry when she married Henry II of England. The Hundred Years War put an end to that, but it didn't stop the continuous trade between England and Bordeaux, or the intermarriage that accompanied it. Many of us have English ancestors in our family trees. I've one myself, way back.'

He had a firm, fine-drawn mouth which Roxanne watched helplessly as he spoke, drowning in the quietly mesmeric quality of his voice, spellbound by the economical but telling gestures of his narrow, cultured hands beneath the white cuffs of his shirt.

She realised that he must be about thirty, considerably older than herself. Roxanne knew plenty of boys, but this was a man, mature, fully formed, authoritative. At ease, and possessed of the ability to put others at ease. But while she did feel perfectly comfortable talking to him, as if she had known him always, a profound and subtle excitement bubbled in her veins. The spacious room seemed bigger, the people in it, the bustling city beyond the tall windows more beautiful, the air she breathed full of a high-altitude champagne quality. Everything was larger than life and painted in brighter colours, and even she herself was no longer the same shy nonentity who had walked into this house an hour earlier.

'You are very knowledgeable about Bordeaux, Monsieur Deslandes.'

'Alain, please, unless you want me to feel about fifty, which I do anyhow, compared to you.'

He deftly snared two more glasses of wine from a passing waitress, and handed one to her.

'I am sure you are not anywhere near that age,' she said daringly. 'Nor am I exactly an infant. I'm twenty.'

'The same age as most of my students,' he laughed drily. 'Now you see the reason why I'm knowledgeable, which makes it less praiseworthy. In addition to being a native Bordelais I lecture in history.'

Roxanne's heart sank, and the bright sky turned dark around her. Yes, of course he did. Even without his earlier reference to the university, she might have spotted him instantly as an academic if her senses had not been so bemused. And he had sought her out, as he would probably have sought out any one of his students whom he could see was nervous and socially out of her depth. He saw her as a girl, not as a woman. How could she have believed otherwise?

She took a large gulp of her wine. People were beginning to drift away, out to dinner or other engagements. The cocktail hour was almost over. Time was running out; she might never see him again, and the knowledge was unbearable. Roxanne looked up into his face, recording it feature by feature on the videotape of her memory, knowing that the memory alone would never be enough. He returned her seeking gaze very seriously, unsmiling.

'What are you planning to do tomorrow?' asked Alain Deslandes. 'Whatever it is—cancel it.'

The message at Reception had been that Monsieur Deslandes would call for them at nine-thirty, and he was there on the dot, cool and immaculate in pale grey summer-weight trousers and a short-sleeved shirt. Roxanne could not help but note how brown his arms were and the skin exposed at the neck of his shirt. He

had always tanned easily, and liked to be outdoors as
much as possible when not engaged in academic pursuits.

'Good morning, ladies.' He greeted them politely, his
manner pleasant but far from effusive. 'I hope you slept
well?'

'Excellently, thank you,' Roxanne lied promptly. She
wasn't about to give him the idea that any thoughts concerning *him* had kept her awake!

'Speak for yourself,' Jeannie grumbled. 'There are too
many old churches with bells in this city of yours, Alain.
They chime regularly, and not always in harmony!'

'One gets used to it,' he smiled. 'Are you wide awake
enough to cope with the visit to the *chai*? I sincerely
hope so, since I've telephoned the *négociant* and spoken
personally to Monsieur Dubois, who is Didier Joly's superior, and happens also to be a personal friend of my
father's. He will be pleased to show you around.'

The significance of this was not lost on Roxanne. They
were going to be hosted by the head wine merchant
himself, not simply his underling. As everywhere, it was
whom you knew that counted a good deal in the scheme
of things. Alain had presumably known Monsieur
Dubois since childhood, as their fathers were both in the
trade. It was unlikely that she and Jeannie on their own
would have received such favoured treatment.

Roxanne had no desire to be beholden to Alain in any
way. But she desperately wanted to do a good job for
Bien Vivre, so for the moment she simply had to grit her
teeth and accept his patronage.

'It's good of you to spare us your time, Alain,' she
said, trying not to sound grudging. 'I'm sure you must
be as busy as ever.'

He shrugged.

'Think nothing of it. Didier is an old friend,' he said
coolly, making it abundantly clear that the favour was

for Didier, and not for her. 'Dubois *père* is a little bit crusty, but there's very little he does not know about wine. Shall we go? I didn't bring the car. It's an easier city to negotiate on foot, and the *chais* are not far away.'

The route Alain took led them through the old Place de Parlement, where café tables, already busy, brightened the sombre grey of ancient buildings. She remembered evenings they had sat there, drinking coffee and watching the sky darken, their fingertips linked and tingling with awareness of one another, and she could not resist stealing a quick glance at him.

But if he remembered there was nothing in his detached, businesslike expression to betray the fact, and his easy stride did not falter as they passed through the square. He had probably written off that part of his life as a brief aberration, a summer madness that should never have happened, that had faded like a distant mirage. As she had also relegated it to the dusty attic of memory, she told herself firmly.

They came out on the Place de la Bourse, facing the broad river which was the heartbeat of the city's commerce and within a short walk of the great quayside mansions built by earlier generations of wine brokers. The one they entered was still called the Hotel Dubois, as it had been when the merchant family had both lived and pursued its business within these premises.

Jeannie looked around her at the immense vestibule with its great carpeted staircase, and whispered to Roxanne, 'This is more like a temple than a business! Do I have to curtsy to this old boy when we meet him? All I know about Frenchmen is that they kiss your hand and say *"enchanté"*.'

Roxanne choked back a cough and hoped that Alain, who was a short way ahead of them, had not heard. He might consider mirth to indicate a lack of respect for the seriousness of the occupation carried on under this roof.

'I don't think much hand-kissing goes on nowadays,' she said. 'And no one says *"enchanté"* except in films! If you wish to be correct you say, *"Je suis heureuse de faire votre connaissance!"* That will make a good impression.'

'It won't, because I'll never get my tongue round such a mouthful! I'll leave it to you,' Jeannie declared, and started to fiddle nervously with her light-meters.

Monsieur Dubois did not kiss their hands, but it would have surprised neither of them had he done so, as he personified a stiff, old-fashioned courtesy along with a permanent astonishment that two young *women* were here to do this job. He was obviously delighted to see Alain, and engaged him in a lengthy conversation about family and business matters. Waiting with as much patience as she could muster for this to be concluded, Roxanne was obliged to concede that without Alain the interview would have been difficult, if not impossible.

However, the elderly man warmed to his subject as he showed them around.

'Regrettably no one occupies these big houses now, as they did in the old days, when merchants lived "over the shop",' he said, showing them the huge reception-rooms whose enormous windows overlooked the river. Most of these rooms were just offices now, but he had kept one as a kind of museum, exhibiting valuable Louis XV and XVI furniture, fragile but priceless tapestries, and other antique artefacts which gave a taste of how the wealthy merchant families had once been accustomed to live in immense style. Roxanne looked down at the shining parquet floors which were in every room, all made of the exotic, expensive woods the city had once imported in bulk, and a familiar excitement began to stir inside her.

She saw how her work would proceed, as a piece of sculpture might emerge from rough marble. The past was the key, she thought as they inspected the cool, lofty cellars where the precious wine was stored, racked, fined, and from where, ultimately, it set out on its journey to the world's tables; the past, and the way in which it was intermingled with the present, here in Bordeaux and in the châteaux of the Médoc which grew its lifeblood— the grapes. The venerable lineage of history and the thrusting force of modern technology to which it was now harnessed.

She took out her small notepad and began to jot down ideas swiftly, as they occurred to her, in the personal shorthand she had developed, pausing now and then to ask a question of Monsieur Dubois, politely but pertinently. For a while, as her work engrossed her, she almost forgot about Alain's presence, immersing herself totally in the fascinating process and taking care to make sure she understood fully all the technicalities involved in production.

'And now, *mesdemoiselles*, and *monsieur*, of course, we shall have a little tasting,' said Monsieur Dubois, the hint of a twinkle in his shrewd merchant's eyes. 'For what use is all this talking if you do not savour the end product, *hein*?'

A selection of bottles was produced and opened. Silent, efficient acolytes appeared, bearing elegant crystal glasses, and the liquid was poured into them, glowing like molten rubies in the cool cavern of the cellar.

'Too much of this and I shall be squiffy!' Jeannie muttered under her breath.

Roxanne could not hide a smile, and, turning away so that Monsieur Dubois did not misinterpret her amusement, she found herself looking up into Alain's quietly observant, all-knowing face.

'*Bien, alors,*' he said softly. 'We have seen much industrious efficiency this morning, but very little of *that*. I had begun to think you had changed into such a super-cool business executive that you had forgotten how to laugh.'

Why did she have this uncomfortable conviction that he was subtly poking fun at her? That he was neither fooled nor impressed by the new, efficient, emotionally sterile Roxanne?

'You're mistaken. I save my laughter for appropriate moments,' she pointed out coolly, her smile snapping off. 'Right now I'm here to work, not to amuse myself.'

'How unfortunate that life does not obligingly compartmentalise everything for us,' he said, his expression not altering, his voice still on the same low, even pitch. 'There are times when we have to be prepared to find humour in pathos, and laughter in adversity.'

Roxanne could feel the dangerous pressure of old, unwanted emotions threatening to explode through the fragile carapace of her self-taught composure the way a hot geyser forced its way through a thin skin of mud. She applied the clamp of anger as firmly as she dared.

'I have no idea what you mean,' she said in a low voice, praying that Jeannie and Monsieur Dubois were still absorbed in comparing the '86 vintage with the '85. 'But I'll tell you one thing: I did not come to Bordeaux expecting to meet you. It isn't exactly a happy coincidence for me, and I can't understand why you agreed to take over from Didier. Surely he could have found someone else?'

His eyes hardened.

'Maybe I was curious to see what sort of woman you had become,' he said nonchalantly. 'Meeting you again does not trouble me in the least, and I can't see why you should be so concerned by it. One might have expected you to have grown up.'

The smile reappeared tauntingly as she gasped in outrage, lost for a suitably stinging reply to this insult.

'Do try the claret, or Monsieur Dubois will think you don't appreciate his art,' he said smoothly, refilling her glass. 'And if I might advise you—keep your mind off personal animosities. Where you and I are concerned, it's all a matter of long ago and far away, is it not?'

And, turning to ask Jeannie for her opinion of what she was drinking, he unconcernedly but quite deliberately presented Roxanne with his back.

Gall rose in her, so bitter, so full of angry resentment that she all but choked, and had to gulp back the expensive liquid as if it were supermarket plonk simply to help her swallow the bile of her own emotions.

Laughter in adversity, indeed! Humour in pathos! It was all very fine for him to be philosophical. Obviously he cared very little about the suffering he had inflicted on her when he had turned casually to another woman and the shock of his betrayal had caused her to miscarry their child.

It had hurt her dreadfully then, and it hurt her all over again now. It was as if she stood bleeding all over the pristine floor of Monsieur Dubois's elegant *chai* while, once again, Alain turned his back on her.

She had thought she was cured of hating him, as she was of loving him, long ago. But she hated him now with a fierce passion which burned as strongly as ever. If he could still arouse such raw emotion in her, how could she ever believe herself safe in his company?

What had she told herself less than an hour ago? The past was the key. The past, and how it affected and was interwoven with the present. If that was true of the work she was here to do, how much more was it true of her own life? She had sought to keep them separate, past and present, work and emotion. But already the fragile barriers were beginning to crumble, and she had nowhere to hide.

CHAPTER THREE

AFTER the tour of the *chai* was concluded Alain insisted on taking both girls to lunch, despite Roxanne's protestations that it wasn't really necessary, and they had already taken up enough of his time when he must have more important things to do. None of this budged him a centimetre from his stated intention, as she should perhaps have realised that it would not.

'Anyone might think we were still a married couple, the way you are so determined to be rid of me, Roxanne,' he said mildly.

The mere recollection of those days sent a shiver up her spine.

'Knowing where you were was harder than getting rid of you in those days, Alain,' she retorted tartly.

He merely grinned and refused to be irritated by this barb, but she was sure he had found a perfect way to get his own back when he led them unerringly to the restaurant on the Rue Ste-Catherine which had been a favourite of theirs in their time together.

Roxanne had no wish whatsoever to sit here, surrounded by memories, confronting the uneasy shade of her younger self, and she prayed that the restaurant would be fully booked, and that they would be obliged to eat elsewhere. It was evidently still as popular with local diners as it had been in the past.

But no, a table was already reserved for three, and, following the waiter to it, she realised it was the selfsame table, in the same secluded corner of the terrace, where the two of them had always loved to sit.

She glanced darkly at him from beneath lowered lashes. Had he planned this deliberately in order to unnerve her? His expression was unchanged—calm, untroubled—and he was superbly in control of himself and of the occasion, but the more time passed, the more Roxanne had the unmistakable feeling that he did still harbour feelings of hostility towards her.

But why? Because she had gone off at a tangent, demanding an immediate divorce without any discussion or attempt at reconciliation? What had he expected? After all, she had been the injured party, and he had given her plenty of cause. Nor had he tried to dissuade her, because by then, she thought, he had been relieved to be rid of her.

She sank into her chair, wishing a magic carpet would descend and whisk her away. At her side, the same vine grew, trained up the same trellis, and the faint, indefinable scent of the young green leaves would have reminded her exactly where she was even if her eyes were closed. She had a feeling she even recognised one of the waiters. The Rue Ste-Catherine, which bisected what was once the medieval city, was still full of busy restaurants, elegant shops and equally elegant shoppers. Time might indeed have stood still, and here, sitting next to her, so close that she could feel the clean warmth of his body and smell the familiar citrus tang of his aftershave, was Alain, the man she had once adored with her whole heart, body and soul.

Jeannie, of course, was blissfully unaware of how Roxanne was affected by this place, and the cruel stage-management of her return to it.

'I think I'll have the oysters,' she giggled. 'It's a pity to waste the famed aphrodisiac qualities, but Gary's going to come out for a day or two, so perhaps I can plan ahead?'

She was flirting unashamedly with Alain, Roxanne observed, and wondered why this annoyed her. It was all innocent and good-natured, and he was certainly mature and sophisticated enough to take it in his stride.

'I couldn't vouch for the lasting effect of those propensities. I don't even know for sure if there's any truth in the legend at all, but it can't harm, so I'll have them, too,' he smiled. 'What about you, Roxanne?'

She thought his brow darkened slightly, his voice took on a faint edge as he turned his attention to her, but perhaps she was imagining it. Why should she care, anyway?

'No oysters for me,' she said shortly. 'I'll have the *confit d'oie*.'

It was an excellent lunch, as Roxanne had been quite sure that it would be. Alain could always pick a restaurant. The oysters came accompanied by tiny spiced sausages, to Jeannie's amazement, but he assured her that this was a local custom. They drank a delicate white wine from the Entre deux Mers with the first course, and, naturally, a first-class Médoc with the entrecôte steak in bordelaise sauce of wine and shallots, which all three ordered as their main dish. All the same, good as it was, Roxanne was unable to do more than pick at hers.

'It's lovely, but I'm just not terribly hungry,' she excused herself when Jeannie scolded her for not doing justice to such fine food. 'In fact, I'm not accustomed to eating more than a sandwich at this time of the day, unless I have a lunch date with a client.'

Alain frowned; there was a strange, oddly tender note to the criticism he levelled at her, and this disturbed her more than his expected stringency would have done. 'You always did have the appetite of a bird, and I see that hasn't changed,' he said. 'Look at you—my mother would still say you needed some flesh putting on your bones.'

She looked away from him, biting back the retort that his mother had said a lot of things, many of them not strictly to Roxanne's advantage. She could not complain that the Deslandes had ever been overtly unpleasant or unkind to her, because that was not so. In fact they had been extremely charming when Alain had first brought her as a guest to the house on the Rue du Quai when she was just another girl that their son was taking out, even if she was a little younger than the general run of his female friends.

It was only when they had announced their immediate intention of getting married that there had been a subtle but definite change in their attitude. Nothing had ever been said directly to her, but she had sensed their disapproval, and it had cast a cloud over her happiness.

'Why don't they like me? Is it because I'm English?' she had asked Alain, hurt and puzzled.

'Perhaps they would have been happier if I had chosen a French bride, preferably from a family they knew, but the English and the Bordelais have been intermarrying since 1152 without more than an eyebrow being raised, so I should not think that concerns them too much,' he had replied carefully. 'And they *do* like you. They think perhaps you are a little young. I've been the footloose bachelor for quite some time, and it's their opinion that we should wait a while. Maybe they have a point,' he had added gravely.

Alarmed, Roxanne had cried recklessly, 'But I don't want to wait!'

'Oh, God, nor do I!' he had groaned, taking her in his arms, and that had been that.

They'd had a point, Roxanne conceded now. Doubtless they had known their son better than she had, and had realised it was unlikely that the inexperienced English girl would hold his affections for very long. Still, remembering those long, stilted dinners in the formal dining-room, under the antique chandeliers which, Mathilde had told her, had once graced the palace of some long-dead prince, Roxanne could not suppress the stirrings of an old resentment. They could have made it easier for her.

'How are your parents these days?' she asked with cool politeness.

'They are well, thank you,' he replied smoothly. 'As a matter of fact, I'm living with them again at the moment. At least, when I'm in Bordeaux. At weekends, and whenever else I have the opportunity, I usually go up to the beach house.'

The beach house. Seventy miles north, in the Charente Maritime, across the mouth of the Gironde, the Deslandes family owned a property in the small resort of La Palmyre, which nestled among pine trees close to a necklet of golden beaches strung along the beautiful coast. Roxanne recalled it only too well. It was where she and Alain had begun their short married life together.

'I would have thought it would be more convenient to have a house of your own in Bordeaux, close to the university and the libraries,' she remarked, remembering all the times pressure of work had made him late home, or unable to come at all. At least that was what he had told her. Only later, looking back, she had found a different interpretation for the nights she had spent alone.

He shrugged.

'Not really, because, as I told you, I'm on a year's sabbatical. After that I'm undecided as to where my future lies. I have various offers to weigh up. I may go back to the States—my university there has offered me

the history chair—or...who knows?' He refilled all their
glasses with what remained of the wine, and signalled
for coffee.

'That means you'll be a professor. Aren't you frightfully young for that?' Jeannie enquired.

'Not in America,' he said. 'It's an important factor,
and one which might tempt me back. On the other hand,
this is my home, and——' He paused, and then closed
up suddenly, apparently deciding that the various ar-
guments for and against his return to the States were no
business of this new acquaintance, and certainly had
nothing to do with his ex-wife.

'It hardly seems worth the trouble of acquiring a
property for so short a spell. I could have rented, of
course, but there's plenty of room at home. As Roxanne
could tell you, it's a large house, so we don't get in each
other's space.'

'I'm sure they are glad to have you back under their
roof,' Roxanne could not help saying as she unwillingly
recalled that house. It would give them time and opportunity to cast the net around for a nice French wife
for him.

The tiny, uncomfortable nuances of this were lost on
Jeannie, who asked curiously, 'Didn't your father mind
your not following him into the wine trade, Alain? I
thought these things were handed down in families, from
one generation to the next, and so on.'

'You are right, they frequently are,' he agreed. 'I am
sure my father would have been more than happy had
I chosen that profession, but he doesn't feel I've totally
disgraced the family. Especially since I took the history
of this area as my principal field of research.'

And all they ask of you now is a suitable marriage to
carry the Deslandes dynasty into the next generation,
Roxanne thought, astonished by the deep residue of bit-

terness she tapped within herself. This was impossible. She should never have come back. At that moment she was within a hair's breadth of going back to her hotel, phoning Toby and telling him he could find someone else for this job—even if it meant handing in her resignation at the same time, which it probably would. Toby didn't employ failures.

It was Alain himself who unknowingly saved her from this course of action, stiffening both her spine and her resolve.

'Tomorrow we have the first of your château visits,' he said, addressing himself primarily to Roxanne, his voice cool and formal once more. 'I'd be obliged if you could be ready for an early start. It can get very hot in the Médoc at this time of year, and, as I recall, you can't stand heat.'

Roxanne sat up very straight. In the space of one lunchtime he had twice succeeded in denigrating her without any great effort, and she did not see why she should submit to being put down by him at every end and turn.

As a matter of fact she ate well enough, if not enormously. Today it was only his presence which had inhibited her from full enjoyment of her food. Just as during that short year when she had loved him, her whole being, her senses and her needs had been thrown awry by the violence of her response to him. She had scarcely known where she was coming from, whether it was day or night, light or dark, let alone if she needed to eat. And then she had been in the early stages of pregnancy, when foods she had always enjoyed suddenly revolted her.

It was during these months, too, that she had fainted once or twice. The pregnancy, and not some inbuilt heat

intolerance, had been the cause, and she was sure there
was nothing very unusual about that.

Bristling inwardly, but maintaining a demeanour as
cool as ice, she said evenly, 'Some of your recollections
are a little out of date, Alain. People do change, you
know.'

'It is to be hoped so,' he returned with equal coolness,
and for a moment they glared at one another across the
table. Then the waiter brought the bill, and he signed
swiftly.

By the time they were ready to leave the restaurant
she had an iron grip on herself. She was fiercely en-
thusiastic about her work, and justly proud of her steady
advancement since joining Courtney and Weaver. It
would be madness to throw it all away.

That morning, in the *chai*, she had instinctively sensed
the format the campaign should take and knew, without
boasting, that better than anyone else in the company
she could handle it. She knew, loved and understood
this region, and she was therefore uniquely placed to
spearhead the publicity which would launch Bien Vivre's
Vintage Range on the market.

Why should she relinquish this heaven-sent opportunity to boost her career and send it soaring into a higher
orbit? Alain had wrecked her life once, and she had re-
built it successfully and satisfactorily. She wasn't going
to allow him to ruin it again simply because he seemed
to take a perverse pleasure in goading her.

Oh, no, my dear and once dearly loved ex-husband,
she thought with grim determination, you don't throw
me so easily, not now. I'm no longer a green girl who
would melt in your arms and weep at your disapproval.

She was a mature woman now, a woman who had
remade herself in the image she desired. A woman who

did not love Alain Deslandes, and would not permit him to break her stride.

She spent the afternoon happily engrossed in consolidating and reshaping what she had learned that morning at the *négociant's* into a neatly descriptive passage, not too long, not too technical to confuse buyers, but with enough information to be interesting. That would be fine for general publicity purposes. For the trade Press she would need something more detailed, more precise, and she jotted out several paragraphs which would form the basis of this when suitably fleshed out.

After working with steady concentration, untroubled by distracting thoughts, for several hours she was suddenly gripped by a fierce restlessness, a need to be outdoors and alone, trudging the city streets as she had once walked them long ago.

About to slip away, she paused guiltily outside Jeannie's door. What she wanted was her own company, without the other girl's chatter, but it seemed mean simply to take off without saying anything, so she tapped lightly on the door.

There was no reply.

'My feet are destroying me!' Jeannie had complained when they'd returned to the hotel after lunch. 'And after so much wine I swear if my head hits the pillow I shall probably fall unconscious.'

Roxanne decided thankfully that Jeannie must indeed be taking a nap, and she slipped out, not this time in the direction of the old city, where memories ambushed her at every turn, but into the bustle of the more modern part.

But even here she was not free from sudden recollections of the past, heart-catching images of Alain and herself which came rushing back from those bygone days to attack her unexpectedly.

Here was the Office de Tourisme, where she had worked, housed in its splendid neoclassical building. Outside these doors Alain had met her after work, his smile warming her very bones and making her heart want to melt at the sight of him as she'd run into his arms.

And she had trodden this same route with him, to the Place des Quinconces, while he explained to her the history of the tall Monument aux Girondins. She could almost hear his quietly authoritative voice, telling her of the regional deputies at the time of the Revolution who had fallen foul of Robespierre. Although at their trial their command of logic had thrown their accusers into disarray, they were still condemned and sent to the guillotine.

'They died singing the "Marseillaise",' Alain's voice came back to her, and she could almost feel his arm around her shoulder as they had stood then. 'Loudly at first, because they were many, but the song grew fainter as the blade came down to silence them, one by one, and the heads rolled, until the last man sang alone. And then, silence.'

Roxanne shivered now, as she had done at the time, at the thought of so much blood, conflict and hatred, where now there was sunshine, peace and prosperity. Alain did not see history as the bare facts of yesterday. He saw it as a continuous process, alive and relevant today, and he could make it live for others. She had been sure his lectures were never boring.

She sat down on a bench in the square, at first watching the traffic buzz and roar past, but soon she became quite lost to it, treading her own path back in time.

Everything had moved so quickly after that first meeting, like a film with the track played at double speed. The following day he had taken her to Lacanau Océan, one of the string of large lakes which fringed the Landes coastline. Superbly organised for the day, he'd had a magnificent picnic in a cold box in the car's boot—pâté de foie and smoked salmon, cold duck, cheese, fruit—and champagne.

'Champagne?' she had laughed, shaking off the drops of water from their swim, bemused by the bronzed proximity of his body, the sheer masculine splendour of him. 'That's heresy for a Bordelais, wouldn't you say?'

'No. I'd say it was an appropriate wine for a celebration.'

'You're celebrating? What for?'

'I met you, didn't I? That's cause enough.'

She had not known how to answer him. She had not needed to answer, not in words, because he had taken her in his arms for the first time, and as his mouth had found hers it felt as if this, too, had been planned for her, long ago, in some mysterious karma. He and she, navigating the cosmic ways until finally they arrived together, on convergence course, at this pin-point in time, this tiny space in the universe. Male and female created He them.

The lakeside beach was small and not known to many. He had chosen it well. But shortly after their arrival a family with two sub-teen offspring had turned up and settled themselves perhaps twenty yards away, and the youngsters were consumed with giggling curiosity at the sight of the couple in each other's arms. Reluctantly Alain had let her go, but Roxanne had scarcely known how to conceal that his embrace had shaken her to her roots.

They had stayed all afternoon by the lake, swimming and sunbathing, not talking very much, simply soaking up the nearness of one another.

And finally the family packed up their barbecue, their lilos, and all their assorted paraphernalia, and piled into their car. Roxanne and Alain watched them covertly in silence. She knew he was waiting with tangible impatience for this moment, and she was, too, although she was tingling with apprehension as well as desire.

The moment they were alone he rolled over, enfolding her in his arms, and she held him close, aware of the beat of his heart thudding steadily against hers.

'This is crazy,' she murmured. 'This time yesterday I didn't even know you.'

'What more do you need to know? I promise I'm not a twice-married father of twelve. I love you, Roxanne, and I'm free to love you.'

His kisses silenced her. They were wearing very little, and it was easy for his hands to explore her intimately. To say she enjoyed this sensation would have been mere nonsense. She craved it, needed it...and yet it frightened her. Already she had crossed boundaries of touch and feeling quite new to her, had given and taken more than she had ever dared, or ever wanted to, before. There had been nothing remotely like this in her limited experience. Without any of the gradual steps along the way, love had come to her all at once, and she was unprepared.

'Alain!' Sitting up, gasping, shaking her head, feeling gauche and stupid, wishing she were experienced enough, worldly enough to take this on board, to meet him on equal terms, she said, 'Please...I love you, too...really, I do, but it's too much...I can't...'

She had been wretched with fear that he would find her foolish, that he would quickly lose interest in her. But he tipped up her chin with his forefinger, and smiled down at her.

'*Eh, bien,* it's all right,' he reassured her. 'I should not have taken things so quickly.' His lips briefly touched hers in a kiss that was light and undemanding. 'You may find this hard to believe, but, although I can't pretend to be a novice, *I* have never felt like this before, either.'

She gazed at him in wonder.

'Truly? You haven't loved anyone before?'

'*Vraiment,*' he insisted firmly. 'I never have—not seriously. But please, *chérie*, put on some more clothes or I shall forget about being well-behaved. Are you hungry? Let's go find somewhere to have dinner.'

They met every day for the next three weeks, and the summer assumed a magical quality. The city, the sky, the very air they breathed, all were invested with it.

But Roxanne was in a dilemma. She was sure beyond all doubt of her love for him. How could she feel this way and have room for any uncertainty? But she was young, green and in a foreign land, she was a virgin, and she was scared of the emotional upheaval of surrendering that status. Part of her burned, increasingly, to make love fully with him, and every day it was harder to deny that need. Part of her still held back, and she was rent almost in two by these fiercely conflicting needs.

Alain was incredibly patient and careful not to intensify the pressure on her, but he was only human, and she would have had to be blind, deaf and insensate not to feel the strength of his desire.

They sat on café terraces under the stars, they held hands in restaurants, they kissed and caressed wildly in his car, or anywhere they could find the privacy to do so.

Even that was not easy. Alain, after several peripatetic academic years around Europe, was staying in his parents' house while deciding where his next move would be—he had already confided to Roxanne that he was negotiating an extremely lucrative and interesting lectureship with an American university. Roxanne was in single-sex lodgings shared with other girls. There was nowhere they could be together naturally and easily, without resorting to the tawdry tactic of booking into a hotel for the night. To accord him his due, Alain never even suggested this solution to the shy English girl.

It could not have gone on indefinitely like this without boiling point being reached and a subsequent explosion. The crisis came when, midway through August, Frederic and Mathilde Deslandes took off for a golfing weekend in Portugal. Alain mentioned this casually to Roxanne in conversation, although, looking back, she had to admit he did not at any time suggest that, since he would have the house to himself, she should stay the night.

'Come to dinner. I'll cook,' he invited her. 'My mother won't have men fooling around in her kitchen when she's in residence—she says they are only dilettantes, and don't take it seriously. Actually, I'm quite a good cook.'

Roxanne emerged from the Office de Tourisme at five-thirty into a white-hot afternoon. The baking sun caressed her skin; she felt young and alive, vibrant with the energy of love.

What on earth am I waiting for? she asked herself. I am never in a million years going to feel this way about anyone else, so what more do I want? I worship him. I'm going crazy with wanting him. I'm his already, in every way but one. What has to be, has to be.

The warmth of her smile as he opened the door to her dazzled him with a new brilliance.

'You look different,' he said. 'Very special. What is it?'

'I love you, that's all.'

'*Moi non plus,*' he agreed. 'Don't stand in the hallway—come on in. I'm spoiling my sauce.'

That made her laugh. She confessed her undying love, and he worried about his sauce! Wasn't life wonderful, multi-faceted, vari-coloured, and endlessly fascinating? She continued to laugh and smile all through dinner, no longer afraid or unsure, wanting only to be a part of him. They danced to music on the stereo, holding each other very close. Then, as he finally drew the velvet drapes across the long windows, he said, 'I had better take you home now, my love.'

'No, Alain,' she said quietly. 'You don't have to. I don't want to go. I want to stay here, with you.'

He looked down at her for a long minute, without saying a word, his eyes searching hers very deeply in an effort to be very sure that she meant what she was saying. That it was what she herself wanted, and not merely a capitulation to his desires.

His grave smile seemed to tell her that he accepted that this was indeed the truth, that if they came together tonight it would be as equal partners in a union from which neither of them could hold back any longer. He kissed her, very long and deeply, and she returned the kiss, a whole world of promise in her lips, her eyes, the way she clung to him, telling him, This is it, and here I am.

And then he let her go, unexpectedly but with great determination.

'Ah, no,' he said, 'that would not be right. And it was not the reason I invited you here. Yes, I wanted us to be alone together, somewhere where there were not always other people watching us. But to be with you, only—not to take advantage of my parents' absence, to... how shall I say?... to sweet-talk you into my bed.'

'You would not be taking advantage of me. It's what I want, too. I mean that, Alain. I love you, and I can't live this half-and-half life any longer,' she said urgently. 'Being yours, and yet not yours. Together, and yet not together. I want us to be... complete.' Taking a deep breath, she came right out with it. 'I want you to make love to me.'

'Do you think I don't want to?' He clenched his fist and brought it down hard on the white marble top of the mantelpiece. 'I want to so much that it hurts. But not like this, Roxanne. It would be so...so underhand, and somehow tasteless.'

But Roxanne could not see it. She had made a momentous decision and keyed up all her emotions towards it, and now he was rejecting her. In spite of the careful reasoning behind it, she could view it in no other way, and the shame and the awfulness of it were almost unbearable.

'I don't understand,' she said, almost weeping. 'For the past three weeks I've been virtually holding you at bay, and now, when I...when I'm ready... Alain, I *love* you. How can you turn me away like this?'

'Perhaps that's why,' he said cryptically. 'Roxanne, there's no sense in going over and over the same ground—we'll only make it worse. Come along. I'll take you back to your hostel.'

She sat numbly silent in the car as he drove her back to her lodgings, partly because she was frozen with humiliation, partly because there was nothing she could say that would improve the situation or throw any light on his totally surprising reaction.

Perhaps, when it came to it, he had decided that he did not want her that much after all? But, recalling the white, clenched knuckles and his tense body, she could not really believe that was so. But where did they go from here? Was this, in fact, the beginning of the end for them?

When he pulled up the car outside her hostel he leaned over and kissed her—a brief, tender kiss of renunciation, which tasted, to her, ominously like a farewell.

His tightly controlled demeanour made her afraid to risk saying anything more. Speechless with pain, she stumbled up to her room and collapsed into bed, where she spent the worst, most sleepless night of her life.

It was a penance to have to get up, dress, and drag herself out into the bright, merciless sunlight of another perfect summer day. Roxanne forced herself to carry out her duties at the Office de Tourisme with an artificial smile on her face and a fanatical attention to detail which was supposed to prevent her from thinking about Alain, about last night, but which failed dismally.

Fortunately that Saturday she had the afternoon off, which meant that at least she did not have to face the public for the rest of the day and pretend her world had not fallen apart. She could go somewhere quiet, alone, and lick her wounds.

At twelve-thirty she emerged into the busy Cours du Trente-Juillet to find him standing outside the door, as he had so often done. But this time he held in his hand a single red rose, wrapped in Cellophane and tied with a red ribbon.

'I love you,' he said. 'Will you marry me?'

CHAPTER FOUR

'You look very pleased with life this morning,' Roxanne smiled as Jeannie bounced blithely into the hotel dining-room the next day. 'It could be anticipation of a day's camera-clicking in the Médoc, but I'd say it's more likely the prospect of Gary's coming out for the weekend. He must be pretty keen on you.'

Jeannie's broad grin widened even further.

'It's beginning to look that way,' she said. After to-day's château visit they had no more appointments until Monday, and a phone call last night had confirmed that Jeannie's boyfriend was flying out to join her for a couple of days. 'We thought we'd hire a car and take off some-where,' she went on happily. 'Oh, gosh—that does leave you on your own, doesn't it? I never thought! I mean, you wouldn't like to...?'

'No, I certainly wouldn't!' Roxanne laughed feel-ingly. 'Thanks all the same; it's sweet of you to think of me, but three's a crowd. You two go off and enjoy yourselves. I know my way around Bordeaux well enough, and I can find plenty to do.'

'Mm, I suppose so. A pity Stuart couldn't come out as well,' Jeannie remarked.

Roxanne's quick shake of the head was entirely in-voluntary. Stuart was a director of a company on whose account she had recently worked. He had taken an in-stant liking to Roxanne when business had thrown them together and had invited her to dinner, since when they had shared several theatre outings and meals. He was in his thirties, divorced, a pleasant and congenial com-

60

panion, owned a delightful riverfront house near Richmond, and, as Jeannie put it, was not short of a bob or two. Roxanne liked him a lot—and that was all. The thought of the enforced intimacy of two days in each other's company in a foreign city was not one which appealed to her. They were not that close, nor had she any desire to be.

'Stuart and I, as I keep trying to point out to you, are not in the same situation as you and Gary,' she said mildly.

'Nor will you ever be if you don't give him the chance,' Jeannie said soberly. 'Relationships need some soil to grow in, Roxanne.'

'Jeannie, I don't *want* it to grow. It's fine as it is. I'm not looking for marriage, or even a live-together situation. Friendship is as much as I want from any man—and it's as much as I am able to offer,' Roxanne said seriously.

Jeannie clearly found this incomprehensible, but then, Roxanne thought, happily for her, the other girl did not bear the scars she herself would carry for the rest of her life. Scars which had only superficially healed over, and had left her wary of anything that might lead to a man's seeking deeper involvement.

To Jeannie, relationships progressed logically from attraction to love—which naturally included sex—and hopefully, one day, one of them would culminate in a permanent union. Gary might be the one or, again, he might not. Who could predict what would come of anything between a man and a woman? Either way, Jeannie could cope with it. Roxanne knew a sneaking envy of this uncomplicated acceptance.

'OK, OK, go ahead and develop into a hard-bitten, dried-up, middle-aged lady exec,' Jeannie said cheerfully.

'I'm only twenty-five,' Roxanne protested with a grimace. 'Middle age is some way off, I think! And isn't it time that old stereotype finally bit the dust? You don't accuse Stuart of being on the way to ending up a dried-up male et cetera, et cetera. Is it all right for a man to live on his own, concentrate on his job ambitions, and avoid marriage?'

'It may be more acceptable, but I'll bet he's lonely, and so will *you* be,' Jeannie remarked succinctly. 'I'm as devoted to my career as anyone, but I don't kid myself it can fill every corner of my life. And I don't like the notion of your being alone this weekend. Still—there's Alain. He can take care of you.'

'Heaven forfend!' Roxanne exclaimed emphatically. 'That is the very last fate I require, and don't you *dare* mention anything about my being on my own! Alain won't want my company any more than I want his, but he might feel an obligation towards me, and that would be truly awful!'

Alain arrived promptly at nine, and they were ready and waiting for him, but only just. Roxanne had had to take time out to persuade Jeannie out of a pair of outrageously printed Bermuda shorts, and into something slightly more sober. This had not been easy with Jeannie's wardrobe.

'It's a château we're visiting, Jeannie,' she reminded her colleague. 'Even though it's a working vineyard, it's still the equivalent of a country house...or even a stately home. Some of these old families have been around the Médoc since the year dot, and are inclined to be...well, a bit conservative.'

'Like Monsieur Dubois, you mean? I thought he was a real sweetie once he got used to us,' Jeannie said cheerfully. 'OK—I'll scrap the shorts if you insist. I suppose

I couldn't borrow something nice and plain of yours? No, I couldn't squeeze my backside into your size tens.'

Finally she settled on a pair of white cotton trousers and a lime-green T-shirt. Roxanne wore a cotton skirt and top, and, since it was obviously going to be hot, she crammed suntan oil and a hat into her capacious handbag. Her fair skin burned easily, and she wasn't going to give Alain any opportunity to find fault with her preparation for the outing.

That was perhaps a wise precaution, for he did not seem to be in the best of humours this morning. He was polite, of course, but she thought he appeared withdrawn and preoccupied, as though he had far more important matters on his mind than escorting two English girls around the Médoc.

So nobody forced him to undertake this task, Roxanne thought irritably. He could have refused. If he was annoyed with anyone it should be with Didier Joly, who had been the one to put him in the position of having to squire them about. But Roxanne could not avoid the impression that *she* was the cause of his ill-humour. Serve him right, she told herself firmly. So far he had lost no opportunity to make her feel uneasy; if it had rebounded on him she was glad.

He set out in silence along the D1 out of Bordeaux, past Castelnau and St Julien de Médoc, but then branched off along minor roads which led between gently undulating fields of endless vines, criss-crossed by drainage canals. In this landscape the villages, occasional small towns and isolated châteaux appeared and then vanished like islands, lost in these interminable green seas.

'Stop, stop, Alain, please!' cried Jeannie, bouncing up and down on the back seat. 'I must have this shot!

Roxanne, it's perfect for the point-of-sale hand-outs, don't you agree?'

She was looking at a field of vines, each immaculate, identical row planted with a single rose at the end, as were many they had passed.

Alain obligingly pulled up, the severe lines of his face relaxing a little as he caught something of their enthusiasm.

'Why do they do that, Alain? Plant roses, I mean?'

'Roses encourage bees, which assist in the pollination of the vines,' he told her. 'No one is quite sure who first inaugurated the custom—there are many claimants—but it has become quite common.'

Mr Know-it-all, never short of an answer, Roxanne thought disagreeably. She would have loved to see him floored, at a loss for the right words, just for once!

'I don't know why we're taking the trouble to visit the château at all, Jeannie,' she said nonchalantly. 'We'd learn just as much, no doubt, if we simply sat here and let Alain tell us all about it.'

The dark blue flecks in his eyes showed clearly, a sign of irritation Roxanne had once learned to recognise, and often the only give-away signal on his otherwise impassive face.

'You are quite welcome to go on from here on your own, if you prefer,' he said with deceptive pleasantness. 'I don't mind calling it a day and going back to Bordeaux. There are a million other things I could more profitably be doing.'

He looked so ready to carry out this threat that Jeannie squealed piteously, 'Oh, no! You won't just abandon us here!'

Roxanne sniffed.

'Don't be an idiot, Jeannie. He doesn't really intend doing any such thing,' she said contemptuously.

'Doesn't he?'

Alain got back in the car and started the engine, his expression unaltered. Jeannie gave a cry of dismay, wrenched open the door, and almost dived into the back seat.

Roxanne stood in the road, arms folded, shaking her head in despair at her colleague. Personally she'd have called his bluff and let him go if he'd had a mind to. There had to be a village in the vicinity; they could have phoned for a hire-car and continued on their own. On the other hand, where she could have proceeded with a notebook and pen, Jeannie needed her equipment, most of which was in Alain's car. It was also possible that the owner of the château was another old family friend who was expecting him to be one of the party.

'Are you coming?' he asked curtly.

Without a word she shrugged, got into the front seat, and slammed the door shut, her lips compressed, her eyes fixed straight ahead. He was detestable—as arrogant and egocentric as he had ever been. Why had it taken her so long to find this out in the first place?

She sat in furious silence as they continued on their way, but could not stifle a cry of pleasure as they came in sight of Château Burley, clearly visible on the flat horizon above its spreading fields of brilliant vines. It was a gem of a place, not large, but neat, square and beautifully proportioned, each corner crowned by a little conical turret, and all built of stone coloured somewhere between ivory and pale honey.

'It's gorgeous!' she gasped. 'Jeannie—that's it! That's the picture I must have for the front cover of the publicity brochure, without question!'

Her enthusiasm seemed to have a softening effect on Alain's dark mood, and his expression lightened as they approached the château via a long gravelled drive and drew up outside.

'Château Burley,' he said. 'One of the many English names this region is littered with, although their owners are as French as I am. Gaston Burley's forebear was an English officer who stayed on after the Napoleonic wars. That story should surely appeal to the chauvinistic hearts of English wine-drinkers.'

Roxanne ventured to look directly into his eyes, and found that, although he wasn't smiling, the frown that had creased his brow earlier had faded. His voice was only slightly mocking, and she did not believe the taunt was intended as anything more than a joke, for once.

'Oh, I'm sure it will have a certain appeal,' she said easily. 'Although, in their defence, I have to say that my countrymen are no more chauvinistic than yours.'

She waited for the retort she was sure he had ready, but at that moment a light female voice called out delightedly, 'Alain—dear boy! I heard you were back, but, *vilain*, you have never been to visit us!'

He opened the door in time to be claimed by the embrace of a tiny elderly lady with perfectly coiffed silvery hair and bright blue eyes. He had to stoop, but they kissed each other warmly on both cheeks in the traditional French way.

'I'm here now, Tante Arlette, as you see, and I have brought along Miss Jefferson, the publicity lady, and her photographer, Miss Nutley. For myself, I'm a stand-in for poor Didier, who has injured his arm.'

Tante Arlette? He had called her 'aunt'. Roxanne allowed herself to be introduced to the *châtelaine* with some puzzlement.

'Welcome to Château Burley, my dear ladies,' Arlette Burley said. 'We are honoured by your visit.'

'The honour is mine, *madame*,' Roxanne replied. 'I promise to do justice to your splendid wines, and hope for a prosperous future for them with Bien Vivre.'

How she managed this smooth reply Roxanne never knew, for she was still digesting the implications of Alain's greeting. For if this was his aunt it would appear inconceivable that she did not know who Roxanne was— and who she had once been.

But she merely smiled graciously, as she would to any stranger to whom she had just been introduced.

'We shall drink to that as soon as we find my husband, who, like most men, is always missing when his presence is required,' she said gaily. 'Do come inside.'

She turned to Jeannie, and, discovering her French to be minimal, slipped into old-fashioned but perfectly understandable English as they entered the château.

'You did not tell me you were related to the Burleys,' Roxanne hissed at Alain.

He smiled down at her with a slightly superior amusement, obviously enjoying her surprise.

'I'm not,' he said.

'But...but you called her "Tante".'

'Didn't you ever have people you called "aunt" and "uncle" as a girl, although really they were not? The Burleys are old, old friends of my parents, who have known me since I was a small boy. I have not seen them in years, but I could not think of addressing Arlette as anything other than "Tante".'

'But does she know...about us?' Roxanne persisted uncomfortably.

'That we were once married? Of course. But don't worry, she and Gaston are far too polite to remark on the fact,' he said with a shrug.

'I only wonder why I never met them before,' Roxanne mused a little sadly. She had a feeling that this sprightly little lady might have proved a friend when she'd badly needed one.

'There are many, many people within my family circle whom you never met,' he said gravely, and did she sense a hint of reproach? 'Had you consented to the kind of wedding my parents wished to give us you might have done so. As it was, we hid away like miscreants.'

Roxanne stared at him, stunned by the cold anger of this criticism.

'Had I felt more welcome it might not have been necessary,' she retorted. Their wedding had been small and private. She had been too shy, too nervous of the influential Bordeaux clan, with all its ramifications, to flaunt herself in front of them, but she had never suspected that he resented the manner of their marriage.

'It's a two-way process,' he pointed out. 'However—it's all history now. Let's get back to business.'

She knew he was right, that there was very little to be gained by raking over such old ashes, and yet she found it hard to be relaxed in this setting where she had come in an official capacity, only to find her ex-husband received almost as one of the family. With an effort she looked around the exquisite drawing-room, and remarked to her hostess on the charm of the small, formal garden outside.

'Charming, but very small,' Madame Burley laughed, 'for we cannot spare land on which vines could be growing, no? Ah—here is my husband, just in time to preside over the opening of a bottle, which is his duty, and one which he always enjoys.'

Gaston Burley was as white-haired as his diminutive wife, but towered over her. He had bristling white handlebar moustaches over a wide buccaneer's smile, and was only too delighted to expound on the family's history while they sipped their drinks. But his great love, obviously, was his vineyards, and he could not wait to show the visitors around.

It was already hot out among the vines, the sun, high above the low horizons of the Médoc, beating down on them as they walked through the neatly ordered fields. Roxanne slipped on her hat and sunglasses, and looked up to find Alain's penetrating grey-blue gaze resting on her.

'So you have learned a little sense, I see?' he enquired softly. 'You would not burn yourself in the sun now, as you used to do?'

'I don't even burn my fingers now, Alain,' she replied meaningfully. 'Believe me, there is a whole host of things I was foolish enough to do once, but have learned better of.'

'Yes, it would appear that you have become very cool and sensible,' he said, so straight-faced that it was impossible to accuse him of mockery, for all she suspected him of it. 'What a shame you had to lose *en route* the delightful spontaneity you once had.'

You were the one who stamped it underfoot, she wanted to cry accusingly. But why let him have the satisfaction of knowing that the memory still hurt her?

'I was little more than a child then, but I am not Peter Pan,' she said coolly. Aware that Gaston Burley was already in full swing on the subject of his beloved vines, and that she was missing what was being said, she concluded firmly, 'I'm here to learn about the wine, Alain, and I have to concentrate on that.'

'*Quoi d'autre?*' he shrugged indifferently. 'What else?'

For the rest of the morning she did her best to ignore him, and determinedly gave her full attention to the matter in hand, listening intently as Gaston Burley explained the happy marriage of soil and climate which made the wines in this one small area arguably the world's greatest.

'It was a fortunate accident that the soil was too poor for anything else,' he laughed. 'Otherwise it would have been taken over and used for agriculture. But it is thin and gravelly, with limestone and sand underneath, so here in the Médoc we have never had to compete with other crops. We are protected from the Atlantic winds by the pine forests along the coast, and our position between sea and river estuary keeps our climate moist and warm. Ideal for the grapes, *hein*?'

Roxanne scribbled furiously in her notepad.

'And the grapes are... Cabernet Sauvignon?'

'*D'accord*. For the most part. And also Merlot. The classic varieties of grape. We also have some Cabernet Franc. It is important to plant different varieties in order to produce fine wine.'

After an extensive tour of the vineyards Monsieur Burley showed them around his magnificent cellars, cool and vast with high timbered roofs, and here more tasting took place. Well aware that they were being offered the finest vintages, Roxanne sipped with appreciative care, noting down her reactions to each. There was so much to learn, and although she was by no means an expert it was impossible not to be fascinated by the process.

This was not a production line, nor even a craft—it was a religion, she thought, recalling Jeannie's apt comment yesterday about the *chai's* resembling a temple. Today she felt like a very humble but willing novice.

'Naturally you will take lunch with us,' Madame Burley said as they made their way back to the château. 'It is only a little something light, as it is very hot, and you must drive back to Bordeaux, but you must not leave unrefreshed.'

'Something light' turned out to be salmon mousse, followed by tender *côte d'agneau*, fruit salad, cheese and coffee. With wine, of course. There was more than enough of everything, and second helpings were obligatory. Roxanne had always been impressed by the French capacity for food, and found this energetic elderly couple no exception to the rule. They enjoyed the pleasures of the table, taking them for granted as an important and essential part of their lives.

'Oh, lord!' Jeannie groaned under her breath. 'It's Weight Watchers for me when I get home! How did you ever manage to live here and not put on a ton?'

Roxanne smiled apologetically—she was simply one of those lucky people who did not put on weight easily.

'I'm a worrier—perhaps I burned it off,' she said.

They were talking quietly, but Alain heard her, and although he said nothing his eyes held hers for a pensive moment across the table.

It had been no more than a light, automatic response to Jeannie's question. She had not meant to infer that her time here had been so fraught, that he had made her so unhappy that she had wasted away to a skeleton. But if he wished to interpret it that way—well, a germ of truth was to be found there.

And then a faint blush brightened the pallor of her skin as she remembered something else. She had not gained weight, but there had been a brief period during her pregnancy, right at the beginning, before it was even confirmed, when her body had flowered, becoming more rounded and voluptuous. During that time his desire for her had increased, and in spite of the other problems that had bedevilled their marriage, their pleasure in making love had been heightened.

His eyes rested on her, half closed, and she was suddenly convinced he was thinking of this time, as she was.

Stop it, she wanted to shout, stop doing this to me! But what was he doing? Her own mind and, worse, her own body were reliving that pleasure of their own accord, her skin was prickling, tautening, even as her body grew languorous with need for this man who had not touched her for more than four years. She had tried her hardest to deny that he was still desirable to her, but her efforts were in vain.

She looked away from him deliberately. If he was in some way trying to remind her of that time, it was not because the memory of it meant anything to him. He was just trying to discomfit her, damn him, and succeeding only too well! Her best defence was to try and hide her wildly seething emotions under a heavy layer of icy detachment, and pray that they would subside.

She could only be thankful that, in spite of her own increasing unease at being in Alain's company, the visit to Château Burley had been hugely profitable for her, and she could only hope she derived as much from the visits she had lined up for next week.

The Burleys kissed each of them on both cheeks before they left.

'Come back as a friend when you come again,' Arlette said quietly to Roxanne as her husband flirted mildly and quite innocently with Jeannie. 'Perhaps Alain will bring you?'

'No—I don't think that's likely,' Roxanne said quickly. 'But I should love to visit your château again—perhaps when the campaign is under way.'

Come back to the Médoc? Visit these old friends of the Deslandes without Alain's knowledge? Could she do that?

Roxanne's chin went up. Alain might be an acknowledged expert on Bordeaux and the Médoc, but he did not own it, nor did she need his permission to come here.

Seized by sudden inspiration, she thought, Bien Vivre are going to need somewhere to give a launching party for the Press, and where better than Château Burley? She saw it all—little tables with umbrellas in the formal garden, a buffet lunch in the drawing-room, glasses clinking, the sun shining, a perfect climax to the campaign. Why not? she thought fiercely. She would have to organise it herself naturally—there was no way she would let anyone else take over at that stage. She would talk to Toby about it when she got home.

All the way to Bordeaux Roxanne hugged her idea blissfully to herself, firmly determined that she would have Alain off her back and out of her system by then. So it came as a shock to her new-found confidence when, as he was about to drop them off at their hotel, he said casually, 'I have an invitation to pass on to both of you. If you have made no other plans my mother would be delighted if you would join us for drinks tomorrow evening.'

Roxanne was shocked into horrified silence by this suggestion, and it was left to Jeannie to reply.

'That would have been lovely, but my...friend is flying out for the weekend—in fact, he should be here this evening, and we are going to tour around a little. Please apologise to your mother on my behalf.'

'Of course. She will quite understand.' His veiled glance fell on Roxanne, and she knew beyond doubt that he was going to put her on the spot.

'Roxanne? The invitation stands, of course, as far as you are concerned. I know my parents will be pleased to meet you again.'

And it really would be impolite to be in Bordeaux and *not* accord them the courtesy of a call, was the unspoken message behind his words.

The last, the very last thing she wanted was to find herself once more in that tall old house on the Rue du Quai, sitting stiffly in that drawing-room, sipping aperitifs with Mathilde and Frederic Deslandes. They had never really approved of her as a wife for their son, and all her visits there after she'd become Madame Alain Deslandes had been little more than prolonged ordeals for her, knowing how they felt.

Of course, she was not now married to Alain. She was simply a guest, who had once, briefly, been a member of their family. They were two highly civilised people, and she was sure they would be the epitome of polite hospitality...

All the same... it could not have been a happy period for them, either, and she did not suppose they had forgotten. She wished she could dredge up an instant excuse, an appointment that would occupy her for all of Saturday evening.

But Alain would know that she had none, and he would see through any story she concocted. He would have nothing but contempt for what he would see—rightly, she admitted—as cowardice.

She shot a quick glance at Jeannie, but knew she could not expect help from that quarter. The other girl had had no option but to explain truthfully why she herself could not accept the invitation, for all Roxanne had asked her to promise not to tell Alain she would be on her own over the weekend. The way it had happened, Jeannie had been able to do little else.

She suppressed a sigh. There would appear to be no way out of it.

'It's very kind of your parents. Tell them I shall be pleased to accept,' she said as graciously as she could, telling herself firmly, It's only one evening—you'll survive.

'Seven o'clock, then,' he nodded, and she caught just the faintest glimmer of respect in his eyes. 'Would you like me to pick you up?'

'No, thank you. I know where the house is, and I'll make my own way,' she said. Arriving at Alain's side, as she had done in the old days, would make it look as if she still required his support and protection. She was not part of a couple with him now, and would rather row her own boat.

'As you wish. Tomorrow, then.'

'Oh, dear!' Jeannie groaned sympathetically as he left. 'Sorry about that! I could see you didn't exactly relish the prospect, but there was nothing I could do. Didn't you get on with your in-laws?'

'It wasn't that we didn't get on. They simply did not consider me a suitable bride,' Roxanne said baldly. 'I dare say they were right. But I was young, and their disapproval hurt me.'

She patted Jeannie's arm.

'Don't worry about it. It'll be fine,' she said with a great show of feigned confidence. 'It's only drinks. I'm not going to be on the menu.'

So why did she feel like a prepared sacrifice? she thought the next morning immediately on waking. 'Drinks' did not usually last for more than an hour. They had been tactful enough not to ask her for dinner as well—or perhaps they did not want more than a token of her company? Whichever was true, it would all be over in no time.

But she knew only too well how much could happen in the space of an hour. In the time it took to drink two glasses of wine, she had met Alain, fallen in love with him, and the entire course of her life had been altered.

Time was a strange, elastic dimension. It sped by on winged feet when you were happy or with a loved one.

It could drag unbearably through an exam, or a visit to the dentist. Try as she might, she could not view the evening as anything other than a penance.

Jeannie had disappeared happily with Gary the night before, so after a solitary breakfast Roxanne went out to find a hairdresser. There was no shortage, but, it being Saturday morning, they were all busy, and it took three attempts before she could find one to fit her in for a shampoo and blow dry. But there was no substitute for the morale-boosting value of a fresh hairdo, and she felt much better when she emerged with shining, swinging blonde locks.

Her confidence took a tumble when she inspected her face. Despite her precautions, there were two pink spots on her cheeks where yesterday's strong sun had managed to catch her skin, and she had to work hard to eliminate them with make-up.

As for clothes, she had brought along the new version of the 'boring black', only this wasn't. It was by Jean Muir, and it had cost her an arm and a leg. It was crêpe de Chine, cleverly draped at the waist and shoulders with elbow-length sleeves, and while it emphasised her slenderness every bit as much as the dress she had worn when she met Alain, it did so more subtly. There was no danger of Mathilde Deslandes looking at her and wondering who was the girl in the cheap chain-store frock!

To add the dash of daring with which she liked to spice up all her clothes she wore large, swinging silver filigree earrings and a matching 'slave' bangle she had bought on holiday in Turkey the year before.

For a sacrifice you don't look too bad, she told her reflection in the mirror grimly as she slipped her feet into black leather pumps and picked up her clutch-bag. The evening was too warm for her to need a jacket, so she went just as she was.

The sky was a symphonic poem of molten scarlet streaked with lemon and turquoise as she picked her way carefully along the cobbles of the old streets. The ancient medieval belfry of the Grosse Cloche stood out, etched in black against this barbaric natural splendour, and as Roxanne turned into the maze of tiny streets which would lead her to her destination she reflected that tomorrow would be another brilliant sunlit day, like so many she had shared with Alain that other summer.

No nostalgia, she told herself sternly. So she had once been madly in love, it had been wonderful, more wonderful as each lovely day had succeeded the one before it, but look how sour it had all turned in the end. Look how they had finished, these two magnificent lovers, in the cold acrimony of lawyers' offices, and the rubber stamp on dry papers that declared that their union no longer existed.

You could not trust feelings or relationships. All the warmth, passion and tenderness that was between two people could not save them from the possibility of hurt, betrayal and inadequacy. Roxanne had not needed to remind herself of this in order to protect herself from further involvement over the last few years. Quite simply, she had not felt able to relate to anyone in the way which might light a spark.

She believed that the capacity had died in her... that Alain had killed it. All the potential for loving with which she had been born she had used up, expended on him in that one short year. There was nothing left for anyone else.

The house was still the same. Well, of course it was. It had stood there unchanged, at least from the outside, for several hundred years. A mere four were not going to make much difference. But its windows seemed to watch her approach, as if to say, 'Uh-huh? It's you again, is it?' and the heavy studded door presented her with a forbidding aspect.

Only once had she felt happy and at home within its walls, the night she and Alain were alone here and he had cooked dinner for her. Even that had ended unpleasantly, although his unexpected proposal of marriage the next day had redeemed it. All the other occasions had been fraught with nervousness and selfdoubt.

She stood outside, steeling herself to press the bell, telling herself that she did not have to feel like that, not now. She lifted a reluctant hand to ring the bell, but she did not need to do so. Someone had seen her arrive, and opened the door for her. That someone was Alain.

Tonight he did not have a warm, if preoccupied smile on his face and a wooden spoon in one hand. In fact, he was not smiling at all. He was cool, urbane and immaculate in dark linen trousers and a white silk shirt, and as his eyes inspected her in her expensive dress, with her impeccably styled hair, the bold scarlet of her lipstick, and the extravagant oriental jewellery, she surprised a fleeting expression of regret which briefly touched his features, and then vanished just as quickly as it had come.

'Come in,' he said curtly. 'Let's get this over with, shall we? And before we do so, I might as well make it clear that this evening was most definitely not my idea.'

Roxanne squared her slim shoulders and stepped inside like a snared animal waiting for the trap to spring.

'I thought my presence did not bother you in the least,' she retorted. 'At least, so you told me.'

'It doesn't. But although I can understand why my parents invited you, for politeness' sake, I find it inappropriate for you to be here in my home.'

The harsh directness of this was enough to make her reel, but she stood her ground.

'Why on earth didn't you say so, earlier?' she snapped back swiftly. 'I'm sure if we'd put our heads together we could have dreamed up a way out.'

He laughed humourlessly.

'Oh, no, *ma chérie*,' he said softly, yet menacingly. 'We don't escape our sins that easily, I'm afraid. There is always a bill to pay.'

CHAPTER FIVE

FREDERIC DESLANDES, like his house, had scarcely changed since Roxanne had last seen him. Lean, spry and immaculate, observant of eye, his greying hair showing no signs of thinning, it was possible to see the handsome septuagenarian his son would become at a date still far in the future.

But Mathilde was thinner, there was a papery dryness about her, a new fragility which made Roxanne's query about her health more than just a formality.

'I am well now, thank you,' she responded with cool courtesy. 'But I was quite ill a year or two ago—did Alain not tell you? He was back and forth across the Atlantic too often for his own good.'

Alain obviously had not thought Roxanne sufficiently close to his family to tell her about his mother's illness. But she thought it might have been considerate of him to prepare her. Apparently he was not of a mind to show her consideration. Her presence here was unwelcome to him, and he did not care if she knew it.

'I'm sorry, I did not know, but I'm glad you are feeling better now,' Roxanne said.

Mathilde Deslandes favoured her ex-daughter-in-law with a tepid little smile, but not before she had carefully and critically inspected Roxanne's clothes, her hairstyle, and every detail of her appearance.

'One must expect these things as one gets older,' she said with patrician stoicism. 'I must say, you have changed a good deal. The hair—it is shorter now, I think? More *soignée*.'

'I'm a little old for flowing tresses *à l'étudiante*,' Roxanne laughed, but she failed to inspire an answering humour in the older woman. She was grateful when Frederic interposed to ask her what she would like to drink. Of the two she had always found him slightly more approachable.

'Alain tells me you are working in public relations and are here to do a promotion,' he said, pouring her a glass of wine.

Feeling her feet on safer ground, Roxanne began to tell him about her work, the Bien Vivre campaign and her visit to Château Burley. But, although *he* listened and questioned her intelligently, his son took no part in the discussion, and Mathilde appeared to be only half listening. It was beginning to sound like a monologue, Roxanne thought desperately, hearing her own voice echoing in the large salon, and she was relieved when a black-uniformed maid came in, carrying a tray of canapés.

'A career for a woman is a very good thing, up to a point,' Mathilde observed rather patronisingly. 'It makes her more interesting as a person. But it may be a mistake for her to let it take over her life. You have not thought of remarrying?'

Roxanne drew in a sharp breath at the pointedness of this question.

'It is a mistake to allow any one thing to take over one's life, *madame*,' she replied quickly. She had never been able to call Mathilde anything other than '*madame*'. 'But, since you ask, no, I have no plans in that direction. I'm very busy, I enjoy my work, and quite frankly I'm happy as I am.'

Mathilde's faint sniff implied that a woman who could not be happy with *her* son had no business finding happiness elsewhere. Roxanne glanced at Alain. It was not an appeal—she did not expect his help—but she thought he might at least break his silence and contribute to the conversation. As it was, she felt as if she were being slowly and skilfully grilled alive. She wished fiercely that Jeannie could have been here. Her presence would have made the occasion much easier and relieved a lot of the pressure on herself.

'How long do you expect to be in Bordeaux?' Mathilde asked.

'Not very long. About another week, I expect,' Roxanne replied.

'A very short visit, then?'

'Oh, yes. But there will be a lot of hard work to do when I get back.'

Better to say nothing of her idea of returning to use Château Burley for the Press launch. Mathilde gave the impression that she would be quite glad to see the back of her, as it was. Roxanne did not see why this should be so. She was no threat, now, to the Deslandes—Alain did not even like her, that was obvious. There was not the slightest danger that his interest in her would be revived.

A telephone sounded faintly from the hall, and the maid came in to say that there was a call for Monsieur Alain. Frederic Deslandes got up to open a bottle, and, briefly alone with Roxanne, Mathilde permitted herself to smile more warmly.

'I expect that will be Elodie calling from America,' she said with evident satisfaction. 'Alain has perhaps told you about Elodie?'

No, but I'm sure you are going to, Roxanne thought grimly. 'Alain has merely been standing in, very kindly, for Monsieur Joly,' she pointed out. 'His time—and mine—has been fully taken up by business. You must excuse me if I am not quite *au fait* with personal or family matters.'

Mathilde seemed more than happy with this explanation. The less Roxanne knew about anything, the more she could have the pleasure of telling her, and she had no intention of dropping the subject there.

'Of course. I quite understand. You are business colleagues only now—yes?' she said smoothly. 'But then, how could it be otherwise in the circumstances? Unlike yourself, Alain is on the point of marrying again. A very charming young woman, French, of course, and *très bien élevée*. She too has a career—her own fashion boutique here in Bordeaux.'

Roxanne remembered all too clearly Alain, at lunch the other day, weighing up the pros and cons of returning to the States. 'On the other hand, this is my home, and——'

And the woman I love lives and works here, was the unspoken ending of the sentence. Elodie was in America now, but her boutique was in Bordeaux, so doubtless she would be coming back.

Roxanne's glass of Graves Supérieur tasted oddly like metal polish, and she could not have said why it affected her so profoundly to know that her ex-husband, who had once cheated on her and broken her heart and her spirit, had someone else lined up to fill the vacancy. Four years was a long time, after all. It was not surprising that he had met someone else. The fact that *she* had not only reinforced her conviction that she had once loved him more deeply than he had ever cared for her.

She managed to mutter some pleasantly non-committal reply, and was relieved when Alain returned to the drawing-room, putting an end to this line of conversation.

'That was Didier Joly,' Alain said, addressing Roxanne directly for the first time since they had entered the room. 'Although he is still not able to drive, he is much better, and will be able to accompany you on your château visits next week.'

The smile he rested on her was devoid of any real warmth, and struck a chill at her heart.

'I'm sure you are relieved to hear this news,' he added cryptically.

'I'm certainly glad to hear that he is well, of course, and look forward to meeting him,' Roxanne said blandly, affecting not to pick up the deeper meaning behind his words.

Would she be relieved not to have Alain's presence on her remaining visits? Yes, of course she would. He disturbed and unsettled her, and that was bad for her when she was working. Bad for her, full stop.

But it must also surely mean that she would not see him again. There would be no reason to. He was not enchanted with her company, as tonight surely proved, and he had a full life of his own, which, as she had just learned, included a special woman.

So why this dull ache inside her? It had been all over between them years ago, when she had accused him of seeing someone else and he'd had the grace not to deny it. She had not come back to Bordeaux expecting to encounter him again, and every time they met it only served to emphasise that their marriage had been a disaster.

All right, she had to admit that he still sent shivers up her spine when he looked at her directly. The accidental brush of his shoulder against hers, his hand on her arm, liquefied her with an unholy desire to feel the hardness of his body moulded to hers once more, his mouth and his hands...she could not deny it. But it wasn't enough, and never had been, and she would get over these inconvenient feelings once she was no longer exposed to him.

The canapés and the wine went round again. Roxanne bit into a savoury biscuit garnished with caviare, and decided that three glasses was sufficient, etiquette-wise, for a drinks invitation. To accept more would be to appear as if she were angling to be pressed to stay for dinner. She could think of few things she would enjoy less!

'It was very kind of you to invite me, and nice to see you again,' she said with a courteous smile. 'I really must be going now.'

They all smiled, formal kisses were exchanged, and Roxanne noted that no one insisted she stayed—not that she would have dreamed of accepting. The proprieties had been observed, and seen to be observed, but over and beyond that she knew, now, why she had been invited.

She had been subtly, but quite plainly, warned off. Mathilde had wanted her to know that Alain had someone else, and she knew her son well enough to be sure that he, with his very private soul, would not have contemplated telling her.

How ridiculous, Roxanne thought, and how totally unnecessary. A sudden shaft of insight pierced her deep distaste, and she realised that Mathilde had never really understood the simple reality of her marriage to Alain. She thought that this little English nobody had latched on to her son as a prize catch—successful, moneyed, from a good family—and she had never realised that Roxanne had been purely a girl in love.

All at once she knew she had to get out of this house very quickly, before it suffocated her, as it always had. She said *au revoir* almost too hastily, and was in the hallway before she realised Alain was at her side.

'I'll walk you back to your hotel,' he said, opening the front door.

'There's no need,' she said swiftly. 'I'll be fine on my own. It isn't even fully dark.'

'All the same,' he said, falling into step beside her, and she sighed exasperatedly. There was no shaking him off.

'There are still some things which are considered correct in France, even if Englishmen have lost the art,' he said, noting her reaction.

'I think I'm a better judge of that than you could be,' she replied haughtily, and his slightly superior smirk incensed her. Did he think that no one had ever found her attractive, apart from himself? She had repulsed a number of advances over the last four years, and was never short of an escort when she needed one, for all she had acquired the reputation of being a 'no go'.

She walked more quickly, so as not to appear as if they were taking a friendly stroll, but it was no problem for him to match her stride.

'Why the tearing hurry, Roxanne?' he asked amusedly. 'Can you not wait to escape from me, or is the explanation for your haste somewhat more complex?'

She paused long enough to shoot a murderous glance at him before continuing her brisk trot. What other possible explanation could there be? Surely he was not thinking that she still found him so attractive that she was afraid to be alone with him?

'I have some reading up to do—preparation for the château trips,' she said coolly. 'And aren't you expecting a long-distance phone call?'

It had slipped out—no, to be honest, she had been unable to resist probing, because after tonight she would not see him, and she needed to hear the confirmation of what his mother had said from his own lips.

'Am I?' he asked nonchalantly, eyebrows raised.

'Your mother was telling me about...' she hesitated, then plunged on, gripped by this fierce compulsion to *know*, even if she did not like what she heard '... about Elodie.'

'Was she, indeed?' He smiled faintly, but did not volunteer any further information. His uncommunicative reaction daunted her, but she had reached a point where she could not retreat, only go forward.

'She seems to think you have plans to remarry,' she ventured.

'And if I have?' he countered. 'Of what possible interest is it to you?'

She gasped. His bluntness was almost too much for her to take.

'Why, none at all!' she declared, a little too emphatically, adding lamely, 'I thought I might congratulate you, nothing more.'

'Thank you,' he said calmly. And that was all.

But it was enough. She had her confirmation, she supposed, swallowing the bitter taste in her mouth. He wasn't going to discuss Elodie with her any further, that was clear, and why should he? She had already been told as much as he considered she needed to know.

All too soon, it seemed, they had arrived at the hotel, and this abrupt, inconclusive conversation was to be the end of the story. He saw her into the lobby, and offered her neither the French embrace nor the more English handshake.

'*Au revoir, Roxanne,*' he said, and, turning, walked swiftly out into the gathering dusk.

She shut herself in her room and read background material concerning her forthcoming trips until the words swam before her eyes, but she doubted that much of it impressed itself upon her brain.

Over and over again the brief sequence replayed itself in her imagination. *I thought I might congratulate you...* Thank you...

He had answered her, but told her nothing. *Yes, but do you love her as you once said you loved me?* she wanted to call out to him. *Does the world dissolve as you take her in your arms? Do you make love to her...as we used to make love?* At last, disgusted with herself, she bundled her papers back into her briefcase and went to bed.

That night, just after she had finally managed to drop off to sleep, there was one of the dramatic, violent thunderstorms characteristic after a build up of summer heat, which she remembered all too well.

She half awoke, believing she was back in the beach house, terrified by the fearful noise, the raw, unleashed violence, more threatening than any storm she had experienced in England. The sky quivered and trembled with a white light so fierce that it even penetrated the shutters, against which the thunder crashed, setting them rattling wildly. Beyond them she knew the savage Atlantic rollers would be pounding up the beach to explode against the breakwater, and the tall ranks of pines would be bending in the powerful force of the wind.

She turned, moaned, reaching out instinctively for the warmth of Alain's body, the safety of his arms, but he wasn't there. His side of the bed was empty, and she was all alone in the chaotic darkness. She fumbled for the switch of the bedside lamp, knowing that the electricity would be out...

A warm golden circle of light brought the bedroom alive and glowing. Roxanne sat up, shivering and perspiring, her heart thumping uncomfortably, and it took a while before its pace slowed, and she realised that she was here in the hotel.

Yes, there was indeed a storm raging outside, but she was not in the beach house, and the electricity had not failed. She pulled her robe around her shoulders, had a drink of water from the carafe on her bedside table, and slowly recollected her senses.

The storm rumbled away into the distance, harmlessly. That other night it had not. It had continued all night, a cosmic show of *son et lumière* that was more like a blitzkrieg. The walls had shaken as if pounded by cannon as the storm had shaken the house the way a terrior shook a rabbit, refusing to let it go.

Roxanne had run from room to room, but there had seemed to be nowhere she could escape from it, and finally she had crawled back to bed and cowered, shivering, under the duvet.

And there, in the early hours of the morning, Alain had found her when he'd come in.

'I set off up through the Médoc, then the storm began, and the BAC was cancelled, so I had to go back and round via the main road,' he grumbled. Then, catching sight of her white, stricken face and trembling body, 'Roxanne? Darling—what's wrong?'

She had burst into tears, and he had taken her in his arms.

'Poor *chérie*, I did not know you were afraid of thunderstorms,' he'd said gently.

'I'm not—not usually,' she had protested, not wanting him to think her a shrinking violet. 'But I've never known a storm quite like that one! It went on and on, all night— and the power was off.'

'That's why there's a torch on the shelf under your bedside table,' he had told her patiently, and she'd managed a sheepish grin.

'So there is—but I couldn't see it in the dark!'

He had held her and stroked her until she was warm and secure once more, then he had undressed and got into bed with her, making her whole with his loving. It had been midday before they'd opened the shutters.

She shook herself impatiently now. The storm had activated a switch in her unconscious mind as she'd slept, taking her back through the years, but what use was it to dwell on those memories now? Alain was gone. She might never see him again. Certainly she would never hold him in her arms and cry out in delight as they climaxed in love together. That was all in the past. She switched off the light, turned over, and fought hard for the elusive oblivion of sleep.

Sunday morning in Bordeaux. Carillons of church bells, swallows darting back and forth among the old grey eaves, people dressed in their Sunday best for church or family visits, or supremely casual for a drive to the beach. All with somewhere to go, something to do, and someone to do it with.

Roxanne sat disconsolately alone, idly crumbling her breakfast croissant, making her second *café au lait* last as long as possible. It was true that, as she had told Jeannie, there was plenty to do and see locally, but Sunday was not a good day for loners. Surrounded by families and couples, she knew her solitary state would feel conspicuous and unnatural.

But it was pointless to indulge in self-pity. She looked up with a deliberately bright smile at the waitress, who, she imagined, had come to clear the table, the only one still occupied, and whom she was holding up from getting on with her work.

'Monsieur Deslandes is in the lobby, *mademoiselle*,' the waitress said.

Roxanne felt the muscles of her abdomen clench tightly in nervous spasm. Alain, here? Sudden, inexplicable foreboding seized her. What had she done wrong last night? Had she offended either of his parents? She thought she had been faultlessly polite.

Forcing herself to relax, she got up and walked, on legs that trembled slightly, out to the lobby. Alain was waiting there, in jeans and a sweatshirt which bore the logo of Yves St Laurent, and, in spite of her apprehension, her senses leapt at the sight of him.

'To what do I owe this honour?' she asked doubtfully.

He flashed the Boy Scout grin at her.

'Don't be sarcastic, Roxanne. It doesn't suit you,' he said mildly. 'I'm going up to La Palmyre for the day. I thought you might like to come along.'

She said the first thing that came into her head.

'You have got to be joking!'

He shrugged, unperturbed.

'Why? It's Sunday—people do that sort of thing. They do not wander around on their own,' he pointed out.

'We are not "people", Alain. I doubt we could spend half an hour in each other's company, let alone a full day, without being at one another's throats,' she said feelingly.

'You might be surprised,' he said. 'Perhaps that was our problem—we never took time to be friends, or other things got in the way. The other things are behind us now. We're older, wiser; we are not emotionally or sexually involved. There is no reason why we shouldn't spend a day together as old acquaintances. But——' again the shrug '—if you're afraid to prove the contention that you've matured——'

'I didn't say that!' she retorted quickly. 'I'm not afraid, Alain—not of you, of myself, or of anything else here. I have bad memories, that's all.'

'So? Four years is a long time. Bury them.'

She looked thoughtfully at him, unable to read much from the steady, level grey-blue eyes. A lingering distrust held her back, and she knew that her declaration had not been the whole truth. At least part of her *was* afraid. Of him, of being with him. Most of all, of her own fierce and unpredictable reactions.

But if she did not prove to him and to herself that the woman she was now could handle these old emotions she would always be encumbered by the vestiges of that fear. In some part of her psyche she would always be afraid of Alain Deslandes, and all he represented, and how could she get on with her life, as she claimed she wanted to do, with those invisible chains forever dragging at her heels?

'All right,' she said suddenly. 'Why not? Am I suitably dressed?'

He looked her over, the slender figure in jeans and T-shirt, a sweater knotted casually round her shoulders, her blonde hair slicked back behind her ears. She thought he gave a faint sigh, but could not be sure.

'Eminently,' he said. 'But bring a swimsuit.'

Roxanne ran quickly up to her room for her bikini, and briefly paused, asking herself, Am I quite mad? Not only a whole day of Alain, but La Palmyre, too, the place where they had briefly lived together!

She pulled herself together sharply. Bury the memories, he had urged, and that was what she would do. Today would be their funeral feast. A grand slam of ghosts, all to be exorcised at once, in a gesture of independence. Then the future would truly be hers.

'Which way would you prefer we went?' he asked as they got into the car. 'Up the main road, or through the Médoc?'

'Through the Médoc,' she answered promptly. Well, why not go the whole hog? She had always liked the little ferry that plied across the Gironde estuary; one more time she would go to La Palmyre that way.

The sudden tenderness of his smile caught her breath.

'I thought you would say that.'

'It's a pleasanter run, that's all,' she insisted, denying any sentimental connotations. 'The main road is always full of *camions*, even at weekends.'

All the way up through the Médoc the fields of grapes were ripening and burgeoning under a blazing sun, the old châteaux shimmered like mirages in the heat, and the little villages were alive with Sunday strollers. At Le Verdon there was a long queue of cars for the BAC ferry across to Royan, and as they edged forward Roxanne was amazed all over again, as she had always been, by the number of cars that could be accommodated, parked on deck with scarcely an inch to spare.

'We're on!' she said, surprised, and he laughed.

'Of course. You always thought we'd have to queue for the next ferry, but it very rarely happened.'

The trip across the estuary took half an hour. There was a small bar inside, but Roxanne was happy to stand on the upper deck, catching the breeze and watching the golden beach, the wide, curving promenade and white buildings of Royan gradually come closer.

Alain leaned on the rail at her side, his elbow almost touching hers. Guiltily she wondered if his Elodie would mind his spending a day with his ex-wife. Maybe she is more tolerant than I was, she reflected. I wanted his every waking and sleeping minute. I could not bear the hours apart from him. Maybe Elodie was more reasonable, and their marriage would prosper where hers had failed. Still, she felt as if this was a day she had stolen, which did not, by rights, belong to her, and this gave it a sharp, poignant, culpable pleasure of which she felt properly ashamed. All the same, she could not suppress it.

Royan was bursting with holidaymakers, but it was a resort of some style with a vast beach and plentiful bars and restaurants, and was coping graciously. Alain negotiated the one-way systems with patience, and, without referring to Roxanne, he headed out of town via the Corniche, the scenic route which wound along the aptly named Côte de Beauté.

'What's the matter?' he asked, hearing her indrawn breath.

'Nothing. I had forgotten how lovely it all is,' she replied honestly, a little, knife-like pain twisting her heart.

They drove through the sedate beach suburb of Pontaillac and the small resort of Nauzan, past sheltered coves and bays of pale gold, dramatic blue seascapes fringed by dark green pines. Memory tugged Roxanne as she noted the precarious, stilt-like contraptions projecting out from the steep cliffs, from where fishermen angled for the *fruits de mer* sold fresh at makeshift stalls all along the coast.

At St Palais they stopped for coffee, sitting out at a table in a small square overlooking the beach. Mums and dads with immaculately dressed tots ordered icecreams and aperitifs, and as they sat a troop of teenage majorettes in short red and white skirts marched into the square and performed a brisk display of twirling batons.

It was all so real and so natural. Why hadn't she been aware of that before? Roxanne thought. If only she had been less intense, able to take things more easily.

Then she glanced sidelong at Alain, his long fingers tapping the table in rhythm to the majorettes, and her thoughts darkened. She would never have been able to adopt a relaxed attitude to his infidelity, whatever else, so their marriage would always, ultimately, have been doomed.

'Ready?' he asked, paying for the coffee.

'As ready as I shall ever be,' she replied a little nervously. She was already half regretting her decision to come with him, but there was no possibility of turning back now.

The road wound inland here, and the pine forests were denser either side of it.

'The zoo is busy, as usual,' Roxanne observed for the sake of something to say, catching a glimpse of brilliant pink flamingoes visible from the road as they passed.

'Yes, it's always popular, and it's grown considerably since you were last here. But, as they say, you ain't seen nothing yet!' he replied mysteriously. And she soon knew why.

Five years ago La Palmyre had been little more than a clearing in the forest. There had been a square where cars parked, a few shops, a bar or two, and villas hidden among the trees. Now it was a flourishing little resort. There were two good hotels, shops, smart cafés spilling out on to the pavements, restaurants already busy with diners indulging in the great sacred French ritual of *déjeuner*, which on Sunday involved whole families, from tinies to grandparents.

'What?' Roxanne exclaimed, eyes widening. 'Stop, for heaven's sake, Alain, and let me look! I can't believe how much this place has grown!'

He pulled up obligingly and let her take it all in.

'All this is only for the summer,' he told her. 'In autumn most of the shops and bars close, and it reverts to the quiet ghost town it once was. There *has* been a good deal of new building, but most of it is for summer residence only, and mercifully the authorities are saying no more development.'

He started the car again. Once they were past a large
central roundabout planted with trees and flowering
shrubs roads radiated out between the pines like spokes
from the hub of a wheel, and there was still a sense of
space and calm among the huge trees, where the villas
were laid out in verdant gardens.

'Are we going to the house?' she asked, all at once
apprehensive, nervous of seeing it again, and of being
there with him.

'Not yet,' he said. 'Let's go to the beach first. I've
brought a picnic.'

She flashed him a sharp look.

'You were very certain I'd come,' she remarked, a
touch acidly.

'*Bien sûr.* My picnics are irresistible,' he replied with
a grin.

Past the small new marina, as yet barely developed,
but already bobbing with craft, the endless beaches
backed by pines began. Alain parked the car in a lay-by
and got out.

'You can find a beach to yourself here, even in August,
but you've got to walk,' he warned her.

Roxanne was not at all sure she wanted to be alone
on a beach with him. It brought back memories of their
first date, and also of the many times they had brought
picnics here during their marriage. But he left her very
little choice, picking up the hamper and setting off down
the sandy track, the sound of the waves already drifting
up to them.

The Atlantic rolled majestically in, breaking on a
stretch of white sand backed by dunes and sheltered by
the pines. It was as lonely as a desert island here, another
world from the chatting, glass-clinking crowds of diners
in the restaurants of La Palmyre.

GET 4 BOOKS

FREE

Return this card, and we'll send you 4 brand-new Harlequin Romance® novels, absolutely *FREE!* We'll even pay the postage both ways!

We're making you this offer to introduce you to the benefits of the Harlequin Reader Service®: free home delivery of brand-new romance novels, months before they're available in stores, **AND** at a saving of 40¢ apiece compared to the cover price!

Accepting these 4 free books places you under no obligation to continue. You may cancel at any time, even just after receiving your free shipment. If you do not cancel, every month we'll send 6 more Harlequin Romance novels and bill you just $2.49* apiece—that's all!

Yes! Please send me my 4 free Harlequin Romance novels, as explained above.

Name

Address   Apt.

City   State   Zip

116 CIH AGNR (U-H-R-11/92)

*Terms and prices subject to change without notice. Sales tax applicable in NY. Offer limited to one per household and not valid to current Harlequin Romance subscribers. All orders subject to approval.   © 1990 Harlequin Enterprises Limited.

Printed in Canada

Get 4 Books FREE

SEE BACK OF CARD FOR DETAILS

Alain stripped off his jeans and T-shirt. He'd had the forethought to put his trunks on underneath, and Roxanne wished fervently that she'd had as much prescience. Her bikini was still rolled up in her bag. She stood there, unsure of what to do, desperately conscious of her ex-husband's splendidly muscled chest with its fine sprinkling of dark hair, his strong arms and legs. Somehow it would have been the most natural thing in the world to reach out and touch his firm, tanned skin, and yet she knew she must not.

'Aren't you going to change into your swimsuit?' he asked amusedly, and she almost hated him for sensing her dilemma. A black demon entered her soul, urging her to call his bluff, to prove once and for all that she was not under his thrall in any way.

She smiled. 'OK.' Unzipping her jeans, she let them slide down her legs before delicately stepping out. She pulled her T-shirt over her head and dropped it on the sand, and now she was standing less than a few inches from him, wearing only minuscule pants and a bra.

He still had not moved, and her nerve began to fail. Was he really going to stand there and watch her strip naked? Surely he couldn't...could he? Roxanne's mouth was dry, and she swallowed hard. She couldn't be the one to back down now. Reaching behind her, she unhooked the catch of her bra.

Alain's eyes narrowed and his gaze was fixed on her with a watchful intensity, waiting challengingly for her to remove the garment and reveal herself. She could not do it, neither could she move her fingers to refasten the hook; she simply stood helplessly, her eyes large green pools in her frightened face.

He laughed, a low, amused chuckle.

'Couldn't quite manage it, could you?' he asked. 'All right—I'll leave you to it.'

Turning, he sprinted quickly across the beach and plunged into the sparkling sea.

By the time he came back she had scrambled swiftly into her bikini. But she was still shaken by a sense of defeat, a knowledge of his power and her helplessness, and, for something to occupy herself, she unpacked and set out the food.

The picnic was pure Alain—vol-au-vents stuffed with crab or caviare, three-bean salad, a whole sliced pineapple, wine, of course. Linen napkins, good glasses. No soggy sandwiches or plastic cups—a French *pique-nique* was something else. She did not look at him as he threw himself down on the sand, still dripping.

'Did Maman want you to use up the left-overs from last night?' she asked cuttingly.

'I don't know,' he replied, quite unworried by her sarcasm. 'She may well have had other plans for them. I didn't see her this morning. You can go for several days in that house without meeting one another.'

He uncorked the wine expertly.

'She did mention at dinner last night how impressed by you she was. You have grown up considerably, she says.'

His tone seemed to infer that he did not necessarily agree with this verdict.

'But you don't think so?' she challenged, lifting her eyes and looking straight into his.

'I don't know, Roxanne. You are no longer my responsibility,' he said bluntly. 'But I do wonder if you aren't still looking for something you haven't been able to find.'

'That's nonsense. I have everything I need,' she declared incisively.

'Everything?' He held her gaze.

He was just the same as ever, she thought furiously. He didn't want her, but he refused to believe her life could be complete and fulfilled without him. Arrogant beast!

'Everything except a seat on the board at Courtney and Weaver, and I'll be a step nearer that if this campaign succeeds,' she said briskly.

He inclined his head.

'Then let's drink to that,' he said. 'Remember, we are not supposed to argue.'

She saw he was laughing, but good-humouredly, without sarcasm, and all at once her spirits lifted and she found herself joining in.

'What the hell!' she said. 'It's too nice a day to argue. Mm—those vol-au-vents are excellent, Alain. I think I'll have another.'

They stayed on the beach until all the food was finished, Roxanne eating with a zestful appetite that must, she thought, be due to the fresh ozone-laden air. He asked her more about her job, and she told him about some of the campaigns she had worked on, not omitting a few gaffes she had committed in the early days. In return he told her funny stories about his time lecturing in America, until she was falling about with laughter, tears rolling down her face.

They swam together, and splashed each other with water, then lay on the sand, drying off. Almost, but not quite, asleep, Roxanne wondered sadly why it could not have been like this before.

Of course, there had been joyful, light-hearted moments, many of them, but there had always been an undercurrent of apprehension, of strangeness and uncertainty.

She had been too young, she thought, to understand the complexity of a man like Alain, the strange ad-

mixture of intellectual and physical, the deeply serious
and the joker, under one skin. She wished she could have
met him when she was older and more his equal, so that
they could have been not so much teacher and pupil who
became lovers, but friends who could have shared ideas
as well as kisses. Then, perhaps, she could have learned
to know and appreciate the man who was with her today.
Was *that* why he had turned to someone else—someone
older, calmer? Not so much for passion—they had that
in excess—but for the relief of being understood?

On the verge of this new and quite unprecedented
understanding, Roxanne drifted off. The next thing she
knew he was shaking her shoulder.

'Wake up, Roxanne. The sun is moving around that
tree, and you aren't in shade any more,' he said gently.
'It would be ironic for you to come down with sunstroke
just as Didier is recovering.'

She blinked, conscious of his hand on the smooth skin
of her shoulder, not wanting him to remove it. Then,
guiltily, she remembered that there was someone else in
his life, and almost jerked away from his touch.

He did not remark on her reaction, merely said, 'We
have to go up to the house now. Apart from anything
else, I left some books there which I need.'

'Still the academic gypsy, Alain?' she smiled, a sad
little edge to her voice. 'Back and forth between here
and Bordeaux? Will you still be living like that when
you are married again? In my opinion it's a recipe for
disaster.'

His voice hardened.

'I don't really know where I'll be living in the future,'
he said. 'But it won't matter. Because the next time I
marry I shall want something very different. Space to
breathe, and a woman who does not depend on my actual
presence twenty-four hours of every day.'

That was too much for her to take without retaliation, truce or no truce.

'And who does not mind where you sleep when you aren't sleeping with her!' she flared coldly.

His shoulders rose and fell expressively.

'Why are the English so obsessed with physical fidelity?' he demanded scornfully. 'Marriage is about more—and less—than sex, Roxanne. It is not an affair, but rather an alliance. I should have remembered that. And I should have known that you would never understand it.'

CHAPTER SIX

IN FROSTY silence they pulled on their clothes over their now dry swimsuits, and, without a word, trudged back to the car, Alain once again carrying the hamper. He had parked in the shade, but it was still like an oven inside, and he rolled down the window as he drove.

Roxanne bit her lip hard as he turned up the drive to the beach house, and thought now, as she had thought on first seeing it, that the description was not apt. She had been expecting a makeshift clapboard structure facing the ocean. What she saw was a large, roomy bungalow set in mature, spacious gardens in a wide avenue, each house well separated from its neighbours. A wrought-iron-railed veranda ran all the way around it, approached by stone steps, there was a built-in barbecue, garden chairs under the trees, and even a small ornamental pond.

'But this is a proper house!' she had exclaimed.

'Of course,' he had laughed. 'Did you think I would bring you to start your married life in a wooden hut?'

Inside there was a large *séjour*—a drawing- cum living-room—a streamlined kitchen, a shower-room and two large bedrooms. All the furnishings were of modern golden pine, a complete contrast to the house on the Rue du Quai.

The main advantage from her point of view had been that it was out of the aegis of Alain's family. Here they could be like any other young married couple, living their own lives.

'There is plenty of room for you here, to begin with,' Mathilde Deslandes had said to Roxanne shortly before the wedding, and her shake of the head had been spontaneous, but quite decided.

Mathilde had affected a hurt air.

'But why not? You need to be introduced to society, to get to know who is who in Bordeaux. You are new here, and very young. It would be good for you to have a firm base from which to establish yourself.'

'You're very kind. But . . . I'd feel strange. In England couples usually set up on their own when they get married,' she had stammered. Live here? Be the ingenuous daughter-in-law, with a disapproving Mathilde breathing down her neck? Oh, no—no!

'*Bien sûr*, but most people do not own a house as large as this——' Mathilde had begun indignantly, but Alain had interrupted, gently but firmly.

'Maman, we are not ungrateful, but I think Roxanne is right. It's usual, these days, to have one's own establishment.'

'Even so, you may well be going to America next year,' his father had pointed out. 'Is it worth settling down anywhere and setting up home, when it won't be permanent?'

'There is always the beach house.' The promptness of his reply had suggested that he had already thought this through. 'You'll love it there, Roxanne. Acres of pine— miles of sand. Endless ocean.'

It had sounded romantic in the extreme, and so it had been, in the beginning, Roxanne remembered now as she got out of the car and breathed in the resinous air.

It gave her a strange sensation of *déjà vu*, walking up the steps to the veranda with him, watching him unlock the security shutters, then the door. She almost expected him to lift her up and carry her inside, saying in a low-voice, 'Will you be happy here, Madame Deslandes?'

But, of course, he didn't, and she followed him inside, noting as he flung open the living-room shutters that everything was very nearly as it had been before. There were some new paintings on the walls, and different curtains at the windows; otherwise it was all as she remembered it. She stood there like a war veteran on an old battlefield, hearing, amid the quiet, the echoes of past conflict and glory.

'Coffee would be an idea,' he called over his shoulder, disappearing along the corridor towards the bedrooms. 'Put the percolator on, would you, while I round up these books?'

His voice was cool—what price now their fragile truce? she wondered bitterly. For a short time today she had believed they could be friends, and part as friends, putting old rancour behind them. But they seemed doomed to be adversaries after all.

In the once-familiar kitchen, Roxanne found coffee stored where it had always been stored. Spooning it into the percolator, she felt a sudden sharp bite between her shoulder-blades, and she reacted instinctively, whipping off her T-shirt and giving it a vicious shake. Ants! She had the kind of skin that came up in a painful weal if anything bit her, and the ants in these parts came armed with shark's teeth, she recalled.

'*Bon sang!* What on earth are you doing?'

She whirled round at the sound of his voice to find him watching her from the doorway. The expression on his face was so strange that it scared her—he looked almost as if he might either devour her or put her across his knee and beat her. Instinctively she knew the source of his irrational anger, for a wave of the same emotion swept her, too, leaving her motionless and incapable of action. It was desire, pure and simple.

'I . . . an ant bit my back . . .' she managed to stammer out. 'It was inside my T-shirt, so I . . .'

He pulled open a drawer and took out a tube of antiseptic cream. 'Turn around.'

'But——'

'Don't be foolish, Roxanne. I'm in a better position than you are to see where the bite is,' he said peremptorily. She turned her back, not caring at all now about the bite, for far more urgent sensations were troubling her as she felt him move up close behind her.

'Ah, yes—I see. Keep still.' She felt his fingertip lightly anoint the spot beneath her shoulder-blade, and, try as she did, she could not suppress the brief shudder of response to his touch.

'You feel it too, don't you?'

He must have put down the tube of cream, for both his hands were on her shoulders now, his fingers pressing into her flesh.

'Feel what? I don't know what you are talking about.'

'I think you do.'

He turned her around to face him, still keeping his hands on her shoulders. Her body felt cold, cold as ice, all but for the two warm spots where his hands rested, and there was no surcease from this icy shivering but the touch of those warm hands all over her.

'Look at me, Roxanne,' he commanded, and she lifted her eyes to his, to see them dark with need, his mouth grimly tender with a crooked smile that was both melting and purposeful. 'It's just the same . . . this . . . isn't it? For all we've tried to pretend otherwise. I don't know how I ever kept my hands off you, back there at the beach. I want you—very badly—and you want me, too.'

'I don't, I——' she began helplessly, but he stopped
her mouth with his in a long, agonising kiss which seemed
to turn her inside out, but was so familiar, so natural,
that he might have last kissed her only yesterday. She
clenched her hands tightly at her side, fighting an urge
to put her arms around him, but he gave her no respite,
and went on kissing her until she thought she would explode. His hands pushed the straps of her bikini down
her shoulders, and the bare skin of her arms prickled
unbearably. She knew she was waiting for this flimsy
barrier between them to be removed, and she gasped out
loud as he unhooked the catch and tossed the garment
aside.

She was heavy with desire as he cupped her breasts in
his hands, his thumbs teasing the peaks to rigid hardness,
and with a muffled groan he picked her up in his arms
and carried her through to the living-room, subsiding
on to the couch with her. And now Roxanne had her
arms around his neck, and she returned his kisses
hungrily and with a ferocity which both frightened and
elated her. Her whole body ached for the fulfilment she
had only ever found with him, which it had lacked for
so long, and still needed desperately.

'Oh, Roxanne!' he muttered roughly, as wildly aroused
as she was. 'Is there no end to this?'

She twisted her hands in the dark thickness of his hair,
straining against him as his mouth found her breast and
his fingers tugged urgently at the zip of her jeans. There
was nothing gentle or relaxed about this sudden storm
of passion; it was a primeval need for union, for satisfaction, which had to be slaked at all costs.

At all costs? Even at the price of taking a man who
was going to marry someone else—of aiding and abetting
him to cheat on Elodie, as he had once cheated on her?
What was she thinking of, letting a few moments of

passion overcome years of distrustful memories? Roxanne gripped the hard brown hand that was pushing down her jeans.

'No, Alain!' she exclaimed fiercely. 'No—we mustn't!'

'Yes, Roxanne.' His voice was implacable, his hands fastened on her hips.

She wriggled furiously.

'No—please—I don't want to!' she gasped, lying furiously, knowing that his pride would make him disdain to take a woman against her will. And, surely enough, he relaxed his hold, letting her fall back against the cushions of the couch.

'*Tiens!*' he said disgustedly, eyeing her with a frozen contempt. 'You want to, all right. I've never seen a woman more eager to make love. But you don't have the courage to follow through. *Alors*—go and put on your clothes. I'm not going to make it easier for you by committing rape!'

Roxanne became suddenly and shamefully conscious of her own semi-naked state, and, jumping up, she rushed into the kitchen, where she struggled quickly into her bikini top and T-shirt and zipped up her jeans. She had never felt so foolish, so despicable, and at the same time so terribly frustrated.

All the things she had thought and said about his betrayal years ago, all the high moral outrage and wounded innocence—and there she had been, about to do the very same thing! He had only had to touch her and she had forgotten all that, so eager had she been for his caresses. Even now she was shivering with half-satisfied desire.

'When you are ready.' He tapped at the kitchen door but did not come in; his voice sounded as remote and glacial as the moon.

Roxanne put on her bravest face, the one she used at Press conferences where, at any moment, journalists were liable to ask awkward questions. She sailed out with her head high, to find him waiting, holding a pile of learned-looking volumes. I shall never come here again, she thought, looking neither to left nor to right as she swept out and down the steps to the car.

They didn't speak at all on the way to the BAC, but, once aboard the ferry, he fetched them cups of coffee from the bar.

'These are for the ones we missed,' he said sardonically. 'You'd have been better employed putting the percolator *on* than taking your clothes *off*.'

She looked up sharply at him, her face suffused with angry red colour. Did he think she had deliberately engineered that scene? That she had set out to seduce him, and then got cold feet?

'I told you—an ant bit me,' she said coldly.

'Ah, yes, the dreaded ant,' he said with a faint, amused grin, and she flushed even redder.

'I should have known we wouldn't be able to spend a day together amicably,' she said curtly.

'So should I if I had known you still hadn't grown up after all these years,' he retorted scornfully.

'If achieving maturity in your eyes corresponds with making love to a man who belongs to someone else then I'm glad I'm still naïve!' she snapped back.

She fully expected a biting retort to this, and was taken aback when he set down his cup and turned to her with a faint sigh.

'I really don't want to discuss this matter with you, but it seems I must,' he said wearily. 'What exactly has my mother been saying to you about Elodie and myself?'

Roxanne frowned.

'In her own words, that you were "on the point" of marrying again,' she said. 'And to be fair, Alain, you have not denied it when I've tried to ask you.'

'I have not denied it because, for one thing, I didn't think it was any of your damn business,' he said. 'Also, it may well come about. But Maman is "jumping the gun", as you would say. There have been no promises, nothing official, no dates set, no rings exchanged.'

'And no understanding?' Roxanne asked wryly.

He hesitated fractionally, and then inclined his head.

'Perhaps, but only a very tenuous one,' he admitted. Reluctantly, she knew, since he did not care to discuss personal matters, he went on, 'I met Elodie while I was working in the States. As I'm sure my mother will have told you, she owns a fashion boutique, and was over there on a regular buying trip—as she is at the moment. We saw each other fairly often, we get on well, come from similar backgrounds. She's thirty, has never been married, having been too deeply involved in business, and I think for her it is the right time. For me, too. If we are going to have a family it would be best not to delay too long.'

Roxanne's heart wrenched unpleasantly at this.

'I see,' she said in a tight little voice. She wished she knew what Elodie looked like, could picture her. Would it be easier, then, to think of her as a real person? 'And where would you live? Here, or in America?'

'I don't know. Elodie has an established business here, but I have to consider the best possible career move for myself.'

'It doesn't sound wildly romantic to me,' Roxanne said drily.

He smiled suavely.

'It doesn't need to be. We are talking about *marriage*, not romance,' he said. 'Elodie is not like you. We are not "in love" as you would put it. We may or may not marry at some time. That's the way it is.'

'I wish you had told me all that before,' she said.

'Would it have eased your conscience sufficiently for you to have let me make love to you, as you obviously wanted?' he asked, and she glared at him.

'Whatever your understanding with Elodie, I don't think she would be best pleased to think of you sleeping with someone else,' she said in a furious whisper.

'*Au contraire*, I'm sure she has better things to do than to worry about such trivia,' he said with light scorn.

Roxanne's guts seemed to contract and twist inside her. Trivia? Was that how he saw that wave of raw, concentrated passion which had almost overcome them? As an unimportant moment of lust? In that case they really did have nothing more to say to one another, nothing in common, and no mutual point of reference.

'She sounds as if she is tailor-made for you,' she said stingingly. 'I don't doubt you will be very happy together.'

'The more I see of you, the more I'm convinced of it,' he said promptly. 'The roller-coaster leaves one feeling less than pleasant, *chérie*. I'm ready for a smoother ride.'

Conversation lapsed on the drive back to Bordeaux. There wasn't really an awful lot that could be said. Roxanne felt as if the day had put her through a whole gamut of emotions, until she was wrung clean of feeling. For a short while they had almost been friends, then the old, long-buried ardour had flared briefly between them. Now they were back where they had left off, with swords metaphorically drawn in adversarial combat. With them it had to be all or nothing. There could be no middle ground.

He left her outside the hotel.

'I don't suppose I shall see you again before you leave Bordeaux,' he said formally. 'I wish you well with your campaign.'

'Thank you.' She swallowed hard, all at once choked and near to tears, which she forced back fiercely. 'And thank you for taking me to La Palmyre. It was . . . good to see it again, in spite of everything.'

'Yes.' He looked down at her, long and thoughtfully. 'We were happy there once. For a short time, *n'est-ce pas*?'

'*D'accord.*' She managed a haunted little smile. 'But it was a long time ago, and one can't go back. Goodbye, Alain.'

She made the sanctuary of her own room only just in time. Scalding tears sprang to her eyes, and she flung herself face-down on her bed, hugging her pillow as harsh sobs tore at her throat, and it was like reliving, all over again, those awful days at the end of their marriage when she had known she must leave him for the sake of her own sanity.

As she must now. Whether or not he married Elodie— and all the signs seemed to indicate that he would—she could never be indifferent to him, never be free of his potential to hurt her.

Finally she quietened down, got up and went to stand at the window, looking out at the quiet old streets. Alain was not hers any more. None of this was hers. The sooner she left, the better it would be for her.

The remainder of the week passed very smoothly, with Didier Joly, energetic, capable and eager to make up for what he had missed, showing them round the rest of the châteaux on their list. Jeannie was raring to go, too, after her romantic weekend with Gary, who had now flown back to England, but when she asked how the evening at the Deslandes' had gone Roxanne groaned.

'Don't ask!' she replied, rolling her eyes heavenwards. 'Oh, I suppose it was all right. We were all fearfully polite to one another, apart from Alain, who

scarcely said a word all evening. I think Madame
Deslandes only invited me in order to inform me that
Alain had someone else lined up for the matrimony
stakes.'

'Really?' Jeannie's eyes grew wide with interest. 'He's
getting married again? Is that a fact?'

'Well, it's more than likely,' Roxanne hedged. 'I
wouldn't say it's a fact.'

'Oh, come on, Roxanne—either the man is getting
married or he isn't!' Jeannie exclaimed exasperatedly.
'Whatever do you mean?'

Roxanne sighed.

'There's this woman—he likes her and has been seeing
a lot of her, although, according to him, they aren't in
love. She has her own business and is in America at the
moment, but she's suitable, and it would be a good arrangement. It would be a typical French upper-class
mariage de convenance.'

'Sounds all Greek to me, but you know these people
better than I do,' Jeannie shrugged. 'I'm sorry, though—
for you, I mean. It must hurt.'

Roxanne affected a show of indifference.

'Not at all. I wish her all the best—she'll need a re-
silient attitude and a good measure of tolerance, too,'
she sniffed, deciding there and then to say nothing of
the disastrous, bitter-sweet day she and Alain had spent
together.

Jeannie, however, had a knowing gleam in her eye.

'Nice try, girl, but you don't fool me,' she declared.
'It's my considered opinion that you are still a little bit
in love with that ex of yours. I reckon, given half the
chance, you'd have him back.'

'No way!' Roxanne snorted indignantly. 'What, me—
go through all that again?'

'It might be worth it,' Jeannie suggested. 'He's some
guy, that Alain!'

'It most definitely would *not* be worth it. You don't know the half!' Roxanne said with finality.

But she could not help remembering those explosive moments at the beach house, the familiar but still thrilling excitement of his touch, the burning need to be his again. Briefly *she* had thought it worth the loss of all her hard-won composure simply for an hour or so in his arms. Because it still felt as if they truly were one flesh, and the wound of separation continued to ache, making her long to be united again with him in love.

Ah, but those were the crucial words—in love. If Alain loved her...? It was pointless even thinking along those lines. Alain did *not* love her.

He had wanted her—of that there could be no doubt. The urgency of his desire, like her own, was not in question.

Maybe that was all they had ever had for certain, and so strong, so overpowering the force had been that it had blinded them to all the obstacles that should have made them pause—the differences of age, culture and background.

It wasn't enough any more, and he was not the only one who had realised it. He would have made love to her and enjoyed it, and so would she, but the aftertaste would have been bitter—for her, at least, for what she dreamed of was the man she had briefly glimpsed on the beach, and the woman she had never been in their time together. Two people capable of trusting and understanding each other, whose love endured even when they were out of each other's arms and each other's sight.

Two people who do not exist, Roxanne, she told herself. Or who might have done, but missed each other by minutes, or by a thousand years. Since it could not be remedied, it scarcely mattered which was the truth.

CHAPTER SEVEN

TOBY was pleased with the work Roxanne had done on the Bien Vivre campaign. She knew he was pleased, because he did not smile or evince delight, but merely regarded her with a reflective satisfaction which declared he was, as ever, convinced of the rightness of his own judgement.

He went along, too, with her ideas about using Château Burley for the Press launch, as did the directors of Bien Vivre when they all met for a working lunch.

'All you've got to do is organise getting a planeload of journalists over there, finding them accommodation and facilities, then liaise with the château owners to arrange the event, oversee the menu, décor, and, most importantly, the tasting,' he said briskly to Roxanne afterwards, watching her face closely to see if she appeared daunted by the task. 'I think you are going to be ever so slightly busy.'

Even before that there was a hectic few weeks of getting everything she had written, together with photos, into shape, organising the printing of the leaflets, the advertising material for point of sale, and co-ordinating the invitations to all the journalists she hoped would attend.

Roxanne worked as never before on this first stage, only too aware that the day at Château Burley was the culmination, and could not succeed unless the groundwork was properly done.

It was work she enjoyed, but even if that had not been the case she would have thrown herself into it, glad to be kept frantically busy. It prevented her thoughts from straying too often to the wide golden beaches of La Palmyre, to the dark, clever, enigmatic face and bronzed body of Alain Deslandes. She could not hold off those memories completely, but she fought her hardest to keep them at bay.

Toby came into her office one evening at nearly seven o'clock to find her still busily checking out her acceptance list and her schedule for the launch, and he clucked irritably at her.

'What's this? You still here? There's no need for you to work directors' hours already,' he chided her. 'Haven't you done all that stuff yet?'

'Well, yes,' she admitted. 'I was just going over it one more time, just to be sure that I hadn't missed anything.'

'You know very well you haven't overlooked the tiniest detail. You've been far too thorough. Go home, Roxanne—and that's an order. In fact, you should take a couple of days off before the launch. I don't want you cracking up, and you need to conserve your strength.'

She smiled. In view of the fact that it was Thursday night, 'take a couple of days off' wasn't as generous an offer as all that!

'Gee, thanks, Toby,' she grinned, and then thought seriously. 'It's not such a bad idea. Perhaps I'll go up to Yorkshire for the weekend and see my father. It's been a while, and I could use a breather.'

'On Ilkley Moor baht 'at.' Toby pulled a sardonic face. He thought civilisation ended at the Dartford Tunnel.

'It isn't nearly that far north!' she remonstrated affectionately, and went home to her flat with a smile on her face and a mental list of things to pack. It would be nice to be back for a few days where shopkeepers called you 'luv' and people talked to you on buses and in cinema queues!

She had planned to finish work early on Friday, but there were several small last-minute crises and it didn't happen that way. In the end she dashed back to her basement flat only for long enough to pick up her overnight case, water her plants, and see that she left everything secure.

On the point of leaving, she heard the doorbell ring, and gave a sigh of exasperation. Who could this be, at such an inconvenient time? Probably someone wanting to involve her in a long doorstep conversation—sell her insurance or a pension plan. By the time she had got rid of them she would be in danger of missing her train.

She adopted a stern, dismissive expression, and opened the door—to Alain! He wore a dark business suit and carried a flight bag, but it made no difference. The sight of him took her back immediately to the day at the beach house, and her heart made a zooming ascent, thudding to a stop somewhere in her throat before plummeting down again. So utterly astounded that she could not find words, she simply stared at him, open-mouthed with shock.

'Surprised?' he queried lightly.

Surprised was hardly the word! She nodded, still speechless, and he said, 'I came over to talk to a historian who lives here in London. His speciality is the Plantagenets, and some of our research overlaps. We had a mutually informative afternoon.'

'Oh,' she managed to say at last, aware of sounding highly unintelligent, but she still had not recovered from her amazement at finding him there at all. Finally she stuttered out, 'I...I didn't know you knew where I lived.'

'I didn't, but Didier Joly has your home phone number on his file, and the rest was easy,' he said.

'Remind me to have myself transferred to ex-directory,' she snapped, summoning up her only true defence

against him, a protective barricade of anger and resentment. Picking up her own case, she stepped past him
outside, closing the door firmly. 'Now, if you'll excuse
me, I have a train to catch.'

There was very little space between her door and the
narrow flight of stairs leading up to the street, and he
sidestepped her neatly, taking her arm in a firm grasp.

'Oh, no, you don't. I haven't come here to be left on
the doorstep!' he declared grimly.

Roxanne glared at him.

'But I'll miss my...'

He virtually frogmarched her up the steps, and flagged
down a fortuitously passing taxi with an imperious jerk
of the head, ushering her inside and climbing in after
her without giving her a chance to protest.

'Where to, guv'nor?' the driver asked.

Alain looked questioningly at Roxanne.

'St Pancras,' she said weakly, and as the glass barrier
slid to, enclosing them in a moving world from which
she could not escape, she burst out, 'Alain—what *is* all
this about?'

'I want to talk to you.'

'But we have nothing to talk about,' she stated
woodenly.

'I think we have. We did not part on the best of terms.
I think that animosity between us is quite unnecessary,
and, furthermore, I dislike loose endings,' he said coolly.

She stared incredulously at him.

'And this is your way of putting everything right? You
burst in on me as I am about to leave, manhandle me
and virtually hijack me into a cab—Alain, you have a
lot of nerve!' she gasped furiously. 'Well, it's no use.
I'm on my way to Sheffield to visit my father. I have
only minutes to catch the train, and there simply isn't
time! Even if I *wanted* to talk to you!'

'Be quiet, Roxanne. You have a knack for creating problems where there are none,' he told her calmly. 'There is always a solution if one looks for it. Think laterally.'

Roxanne's only thought was that in five minutes, if the taxi made it in time—and she prayed that it would—she would be on the train, speeding away from him. That would be the best possible solution for her. But at the station Alain paid the driver, tipping him heavily, bought a platform ticket from the machine and, still holding Roxanne by the arm, hustled her on to the platform.

The train was there, all ready to leave, doors being slammed, the guard about to blow his whistle. Thank goodness! With a sharp jerk she freed her arm and leapt on board, blurting out, 'Goodbye, Alain—I have to go.'

The ploy didn't work, because with equal speed and agility he followed her example, and then he was alongside her as the train rattled out of the station. She had not escaped. There *was* no escape.

'Let's find a compartment,' he suggested cheerfully, for all the world as though this were an excursion they had planned together.

'This is mad!' she expostulated as he followed her down the corridor. 'You haven't even got a ticket!'

'Then I shall buy one,' he said, unperturbed. 'Look— here's a vacant carriage.'

'It's first class. I'm travelling second,' she muttered stubbornly.

'It doesn't matter. Get in. I'll sort all that out,' he said, holding the door.

Roxanne was incapable of arguing further with him. The train was travelling swiftly now, past a vista of long suburban gardens; it was the InterCity, next stop Reading, and, short of her jumping out or pulling the communication cord, there was no way she could escape from this situation. She subsided sullenly into the plush-seated window corner, and watched as he smoothly negotiated the tickets with the uniformed collector.

'Thank you very much. And at what time will the dining-car be open?' he asked. 'I should like two tickets for dinner as well.'

'Dinner will be served from seven-thirty, sir, but the bar is open now,' he was respectfully informed.

'Good. I could use a drink,' he said, turning back to Roxanne.

'*Moi non plus!*' she exclaimed instinctively and with great feeling, and to her intense indignation he actually grinned. How could he find this remotely amusing? And what *was* all this about? Hadn't he subjected her to enough anguish while she was in France, without coming over here and putting her through the agony all over again?

He organised stiff gin and tonics, which they sat sipping in their carriage as the Home Counties flashed past.

'You said you wanted to talk,' she said stonily.

He shook his head.

'Tch, tch! Decent conversation on an empty stomach is impossible. Relax and enjoy your drink.'

Relax? How could she come even close to such an enviably civilised state with him sitting opposite her, regarding her in that vaguely amused, all-knowing manner? She only wished she had an inkling of what game he was playing, why he had sought her out at all, and especially why he had insisted on taking the train with her. The unfriendly nature of their parting could not have troubled him so much. After all, he had done with her and was planning a new life with someone else.

And yet—he was here. Why would he go to all this trouble for no reason? As ever, she could not completely make him out, and the inability to do so left her profoundly disturbed.

As they sat in the gently swaying dining-car later, eating Dover sole and drinking white Sancerre, it seemed to her that, far from wanting to straighten things out, he was deliberately avoiding discussing anything serious. He told her about his meeting with the English historian, a well-known personage Roxanne had occasionally seen on erudite television programmes, and expounded on the ramifications of the Plantagenet dynasty, drawing elaborate family trees on the backs of paper napkins.

But, in spite of herself, she was drawn out, interested, and found herself asking questions and making points. In spite of herself, she was beginning to relax, just as he had told her to do, as over coffee and brandy they crossed that indefinable but very real frontier where the north began. It was dark as the train slid into Sheffield Midland Station, and Roxanne shook her head as they gathered up their luggage.

'Now what? We're here, and we haven't really talked about anything except Richard III and the Nevilles,' she said with attempted lightness. 'I'm impressed by your grasp of English history, but is it relevant?'

His smile was mysterious.

'It could be. Richard's marriage to Anne Neville was another much misunderstood union, and in my opinion the man had a bad press. There's no real evidence he killed those princes in the Tower, and your Shakespeare was writing for the other side of the argument.'

'Huh! That may be, but you surely aren't trying to claim that *you* were misunderstood?' she sniffed dubiously. 'Not by me, *mon brave*!'

He refused to respond to this provocation.

'Right now I'm trying to put you in a taxi to go to your father,' he said. She hesitated, looking at him doubtfully. Crazy as it seemed, she was reluctant, now, to leave him.

'And you? What will you do?'

'I shall find myself a hotel, of which there is sure to be no shortage,' he replied levelly.

'But——'

'I'll phone you tomorrow,' he said.

Still she paused, unsure and unwilling, and he propelled her gently but commandingly towards the taxi rank.

'It's getting late, *ma chérie. A demain.*'

The last she saw was his dark face, unsmiling but tender, his hand raised in salute, as the taxi drove out of the forecourt.

It was very strange, if oddly comforting, to wake up again in her childhood bedroom. The same paper on the walls—Dad wasn't too keen on decorating. The same trees in the garden outside, making patterns on the curtains. The bed was against the window, and, kneeling up, Roxanne peered out, to see her father pottering around his greenhouse, puffing contentedly on a cigarette.

She pulled on the dressing-gown that always hung behind the door, went downstairs and out into the garden. The morning was warm and full of birdsong.

'Didn't think you'd be awake yet,' her father said. 'Kettle's boiled if you want some tea.'

'I'll make it if you promise to put that cigarette out. It's bad for you,' she told him.

He smiled. 'Too late to stop now.' But he stubbed it out none the less and followed her into the kitchen.

Roxanne made the tea and handed him his mug. Last night they had chatted only briefly before going to bed, and she had said nothing about the train journey with her ex-husband. Now she said briefly, 'Alain's here.'

'Oh, aye?' He looked at her phlegmatically from beneath bushy grey eyebrows scarcely raised. 'Is he, now? And what might *he* want?'

'I'm not sure. To talk to me, or so he says. He turned up just as I was about to catch the train, and decided to come with me.'

Tom Jefferson regarded his daughter thoughtfully, showing no outward emotional reaction to this news.

'Did he, now?' he said. 'Well, since you never told me the full story behind your break-up, I don't suppose there's much use in asking you what this is about now?'

'I'd tell you if I knew myself,' Roxanne answered ruefully. 'I saw a little of him while I was working in France, and it wasn't very amicable. Now he says he doesn't want us to part in an unfriendly manner.'

She took a deep breath.

'I think he's clearing the decks, emotionally speaking. He's considering remarriage.'

'Hm.' Her father digested this news with the same reflective calm characteristic of him. He rarely showed his deeper feelings—a trait he shared with Alain, she realised. 'Well—you're a grown woman, so I'll say only one thing, and then I'll shut up. Be careful, lass. He hurt you once. Don't go looking for a second helping.'

'I won't,' Roxanne promised him with considerable feeling. 'You don't have to worry. Now—how about some breakfast? Bacon and eggs, black pudding? A real Yorkshire fry-up!'

But as the day passed it didn't look as if she was in any danger from Alain, and she began to wonder if he had changed his mind and caught the first train back to

London. It would, however, be totally unlike him. He had said that he would phone, and he usually carried out his stated intentions. Why should this strange man come all the way here with her on the train, merely to return again, having achieved nothing? It simply did not make sense.

Roxanne spent most of the day in the garden with her father, since the weather was so fine. She helped him in the greenhouse, dead-headed his roses, and generally fetched and carried at his bidding. But all the time her ears were strained for the sound of the telephone.

'You'll have no trouble hearing it out here if it rings,' her father said drily, and it was useless denying that she had been listening out. He knew her too well to be deceived.

'It isn't that important to me whether he phones or not,' she insisted. 'But it just isn't like Alain to promise something and not to do it.'

'How do you know any more? People can change,' he warned her.

'Not Alain,' she insisted. The longer she waited, the more important it became that he did ring, and the more anxious she was to hear whatever he had intended to say to her. And, more than that, it came to her with a sense of shock that if he went back to France without her seeing him again she would be... well, disappointed was not a strong enough word. She would feel as if she had been cheated of something vital. This was a dangerous emotion, she knew, but there was nothing she could do about it. It was honestly felt, and undeniable.

At last, at about four o'clock, the phone rang.

'Ask not for whom the bell tolls,' Tom misquoted drily from beneath raised eyebrows. But his daughter was already in the hall.

'Good afternoon. Did you sleep well last night?' her ex-husband asked with polite formality.

'Extremely well, thank you, but I was beginning to think *you* had gone back to London,' she replied pointedly. 'You certainly took your time.'

'Would it have troubled you if I had?' The voice was dry, cool, but carried a soft insinuation that made her tremble.

'It always troubles me when people act out of character!' she retorted, and was rewarded by a chuckle of appreciation.

'That's my girl! But I didn't do any such thing. I said I would phone, and I have,' he pointed out. 'Since you came to Sheffield to see your father, I did not think it right to intrude on your day with him. Good manners are also part of my character, wouldn't you say?'

'Modesty certainly isn't,' Roxanne bit back, and heard him laugh softly again.

'Not *false* modesty,' he corrected her, and then, with an abrupt swing of subject which caught her unprepared, 'Will you meet me this evening?'

'If you wish,' she said, reluctant to sound at all eager.

'I wish. What time do you eat dinner?'

'We're usually quite early up here. About six.' She hesitated. 'Would you like to join us?'

'Thank you, but no. I think both you and your father would find that awkward,' he declined gravely, and she was vaguely irritated by the inference that he, more sophisticated than they, would take such an occasion in his stride. He certainly hadn't been a beacon of sociability at his mother's drinks evening!

'I'll see you about seven,' he suggested.

'Very well. Where shall we meet? In the city centre somewhere?' She continued to play this stilted little game as if they were strangers who had never shared a bed, a home and a life.

'But, of course, I shall come to your house,' he said promptly. Did you think I would chicken out completely, where you did not? was the underlying challenge, and she was obliged to accord him a reluctant respect.

She gave him the address, remembering that he had never been here before, and that the two men had only met when her father had flown out to Bordeaux for her wedding. By seven o'clock she had cooked dinner, cleared up, and was ready, wearing the one change of clothes she had brought with her, a navy blue summer dress with a white sailor collar.

'You certainly haven't wasted any time,' Tom observed laconically.

Roxanne shrugged. 'Alain will be here at seven o'clock, *pile*—on the dot,' she said. 'He's rarely late for an arranged appointment.'

And hated it when others were. Although it had been a different matter when he was working in Bordeaux and she was alone at La Palmyre. Then she had come to expect and dread his phone calls telling her he would be several hours later than anticipated, or unable to come home that night at all.

'Academics' wives have to get used to these vagaries— research is not a nine-to-five business, nor are students' problems,' he had told her. 'You *know* I will be home as soon as possible. Does it matter exactly when?'

Yes, it had mattered—to her, at least. She had found life in La Palmyre idyllic when he was there, lonely when he wasn't. There were a number of holiday people around, but they came and went, mostly at weekends, leaving their villas unoccupied during the week. The houses were well separated, and it was not easy to get into conversation with one's neighbours. One saw them on the beach, or in the cafés, but, of course, they were in couples or family groups, one said *'Ça va?'* and that was it. Moreover, Roxanne had been at the stage where she'd wanted her husband exclusively.

Sometimes she'd thought it would have been better if she had stayed in Bordeaux and continued to work at the Tourist Office. But her time there had been due to expire in September anyhow, and it would not have been easy for her to find a suitable job. Alain had wanted her to be free when he was, and, to be fair, she had wanted that, too, in the beginning. She had not realised how large a slice of his life was occupied by his work.

'Perhaps,' she had said to him one Sunday as they'd lain on the beach early in October, when it was still fine and warm but most of the holiday people had gone, not to return in strength before the spring, 'perhaps we should start a family.'

It had been no more than a casual, half-meant remark, thrown out more to provoke a reaction than as a serious suggestion, but Alain had rolled over and sat upright, looking at her a little sharply.

'So soon? Surely not,' he had protested. 'We have scarcely had time to be a couple yet, and you are very young. You don't really want a baby yet, do you? I don't think I am ready to share you.'

'But I have to share *you* all the time. With your work,' she had pointed out.

'Mais ça c'est different! All wives have to do that,' he had said, frowning, genuinely not understanding the problem. Then he had smiled and taken her in his arms. 'You have me now—all of me. Let's go home.'

We never talked our problems through, she thought now, preparing coffee in her father's kitchen. We simply went to bed and made love, and it was so blissful that it seemed that all the problems were insignificant. Two people who were lucky enough to feel as they did, who had so much love, should not trouble themselves with little difficulties. But in the end it was not the little difficulties but the one greater one which had finished them.

Alain arrived by taxi precisely at seven, just as she carried the tray with the coffee-pot and cups through to the lounge. She let her father answer the door, and did not see the two men greet each other in the hall, but they sat and drank coffee, each behaving with perfect civility to the other, and talking about nothing that could be construed as remotely personal.

None the less she was relieved when Alain said, 'I hope you won't mind if I take Roxanne away from you for a short walk? There are a few things we should like to discuss.'

Tom looked measuringly at the stranger who had once been his son-in-law, and seemed to reach some inner conclusion.

'Go ahead, lad,' he said easily. 'There's a football match I'm going to watch on TV, and then I've the garden to water. Shouldn't think it'll rain tonight.'

Roxanne's lips twitched as she preceded her ex-husband down the path. She suspected it was the first time in years, if ever, that Alain Deslandes had been addressed as 'lad'.

'There's Hillsborough Park at the end of the road,' she said. 'Will that do?'

'It sounds fine to me.' He fell into step beside her. 'I like your father. It's rather a pity I never got to know him.'

She cast him a swift sidelong glance as they passed through the park gate.

'A lot of things are a pity. It's senseless dwelling on them, don't you agree?'

'Only up to a point, Roxanne,' he replied soberly. 'Sometimes it is necessary to dwell on them in order to be done with them.'

They walked past a fine old mansion which now housed the local public library, and down a tree-shaded rise to an ornamental lake graced by ducks and geese. Roxanne felt herself tangibly gripped by an immense sadness. She knew what was coming. What she did not understand was why it should induce in her such a sharp, fierce melancholy that was almost akin to grief.

'You mean, "The King is Dead. Long live the King!''? Or Queen, as the case may be,' she murmured, deliberately sardonic. 'I don't know why you should need me to give my blessing on your remarriage, Alain, or why you should feel guilty about it.'

'Guilty?' His voice sounded startled, indignant. 'You have hold of the wrong end of the stick, *chérie*. That was not what I meant at all.'

'Then I don't understand,' she said bluntly. 'And please stop calling me *"chérie"*.'

'Force of habit.' He sat down on a bench overlooking the lake, indicating that she should join him, and after a brief pause she did so. The sun began to dip below the trees, but the sky was still light. Two boys raced past on bikes, as she had done herself as a child. Among the geese a dispute arose; wings flapped and there were outraged squawks, before all settled down peacefully again. 'Quarrelsome creatures,' Alain smiled faintly, and she wasn't sure if he referred to the birds or themselves.

Then he said, 'I had not expected to see you again, but when Didier asked me to meet this PR person at the airport, and the name was yours, it seemed like an omen. I had no desire to do it, but I thought I should.'

'Well, I wasn't even asked what I wanted,' she flared back, slightly angered by his unflattering honesty. 'But if you want my opinion it would have been far better if you had not!'

'No, Roxanne.' He shook his head in mild reproof. 'You still go off like a fire-cracker at anything which upsets or annoys you. Why don't you *listen* to what I am trying to say?'

His voice was very quiet, but full of an absolute, commanding gravity, and suddenly her breath caught in her throat. She perceived that they had reached a point of vital significance in both their lives, and whether or not she wanted this close mutual examination, whether or not she liked what he had to say, it was necessary—no, it was crucial that she went with him along this stony road. To refuse would be to pretend there had never been anything between them but lust and moonshine.

'All right,' she said, in a small but very firm voice, 'I'm listening.'

'It seems to me,' he said, 'that our life together is like a piece of tapestry which has not been properly finished off, and unless the knots at the back are tied it will start to unravel itself, and end up as nothing but a mess.'

'Maybe it was—and is—a mess, Alain,' she said. 'There is nothing we can do but turn our backs on it and start a fresh pattern.'

'We can't,' he said. 'To use a fresh metaphor, we have to close one chapter before we begin another—and we never truly did that. It's all up in the air. We have— we are—unfinished business. Until we can finally put it all behind us, forgetting the bitterness, the resentment, how can we hope to get on with our lives in a personal sense?'

She stared at him, unbelieving. A minute ago she had reached out, mentally, to help grasp a peace that was eluding both of them. Now, far from forgetting the bitterness, she was reliving anew all the hurt she had once suffered at his hands.

'This is good, Alain,' she said tautly. 'You want me to absolve you so you can go ahead and marry Elodie? You want me off your conscience once and for all?'

His mouth tightened into a hard line, and she saw the warning flags, the once-familiar dark blue flecks in his narrowed eyes.

'Absolve?' he repeated scornfully. 'My conscience is no murkier than yours, *madame*! You ran off and left me like a spoilt child! You wouldn't meet me, you wouldn't talk, you wouldn't even try to see if we had anything left to salvage!'

Her own eyes darkened with pain and anger.

'You let me go without too much argument. I don't recall your coming after me!' she said accusingly.

'You'd had a miscarriage. I thought you were acting irrationally, and once you felt stronger, calmer, you would come back so we could at least talk,' he replied. 'All I got was a communication from your lawyer demanding an unconditional and immediate divorce. You surely did not expect me to run after you and beg you to come back after that?'

'Certainly I didn't!' Her hands were clenched tightly, her face chalk-white. 'I knew you didn't want me back at all by then. You were off to the US faster than Concorde!'

He reached out and gripped the tops of her arms, where the flesh was tender, so hard that she winced with pain.

'What if I did? The offer came through at the right moment, and it clinched my decision. I went, as much to get away from everywhere we had once been together as anything else,' he said harshly. 'Did you think I wasn't hurt by the way you turned your back on me so easily? Lord, Roxanne, did you think I didn't suffer?'

She could not tear her eyes from his face. The pain that twisted it, the fierce anger in his voice—she could have sworn they were real. But he must know now, as he'd known then, why she'd left him, and why she could not have gone back.

'Easily?' she echoed him incredulously. 'There was nothing easy about it! I was the one who suffered! I was the one who lost my baby—the baby you never really wanted anyhow!'

'The one you tricked me into giving you,' he reminded her. 'And you are wrong—I *did* want it once I got used to the idea. I would have preferred to have been consulted first, that's all.'

She tried to shake herself free, but failed. His grip was too firm, too sure.

'I did *not* trick you!' She was almost sobbing now, all vestiges of composure ebbing away from her. 'I just forgot to take my Pill—it was after we'd had an argument, and then... and then...'

'Go on,' he said, his face so dark and forbidding that it scared her. 'And then we had one of our ecstatic reconciliations, and you were so carried away by passion that you forgot to take the wretched Pill. That was your story.'

'It's the truth!' She struggled, and he crushed her to him, one arm firm in the small of her back, the other hand forcing her chin upwards so that her mouth was dangerously close to his. 'Alain, stop it—let me go! People are watching.'

'No, they aren't. They've all gone home. Even the geese have settled down for the night.'

He was right. They were quite alone, and she knew that he was going to kiss her, forcibly if necessary, and she could not stop him. He was angry and vengeful—quite unjustifiably, to her mind, but it made no difference. He was out to humiliate her by emphasising her helplessness, and she knew how merciless he could be.

But when his mouth came down on hers it was not hard and punitive at all. It was firm and purposeful, but very tender; his hold on her relaxed so that she stayed in the circle of his arms of her own volition, her own arms sliding around his neck as she gave a long sigh of capitulation. Nothing either of them said or did made any difference. This would not go away.

Only when he released her lips she found she was shaking with disgust at her own weakness.

'That's all we ever had, Alain—sex!' she exclaimed. 'And even then I wasn't enough for you! You had to destroy me by finding someone else!'

He gave a short, disdainful shake of the head.

'I am not going to lower myself by even answering that,' he said contemptuously. 'It's a mere smokescreen, and you know it now, just as well as you knew it at the time. The bottom line is that you still want me, every bit as much as I want you, and you cannot deny it.'

She jumped to her feet. Even after so long he still refused categorically to admit his infidelity, or to offer any defence, any apology for it. She was supposed to accept it as his right, as just one of those things that happened—perhaps even to take the blame for having driven him into another woman's arms! Because they still desired one another that was supposed to make everything all right!

'The bottom line is that I never want to see you again,' she declared roundly. 'You are not the only one who has someone else. There's a man I'm involved with—Stuart—who's serious about me.'

Even as she said the words she knew that there was truth behind them, that this statement was not a mere fabrication she had trumped up to fling at Alain. Stuart *was* serious—even if she was not. He wanted more than her friendship.

Alain shrugged.

'Really?' he said scornfully. 'I hope he's aware that marriage to you will be no easy option.'

'For him there would be no problem,' Roxanne flared. 'He's kind and caring, and would never cheat on me, or treat me as you did! With him I would be happy.'

So saying, she turned her back and walked away swiftly, picking up speed until she was virtually running as she approached the park gates. She did not look round, but, since she was sure he could have caught up with her had he wanted, she had to assume he had taken her parting line as the last word, and decided not to follow her.

She was so confused that she could not honestly have said whether she wanted him to or not.

CHAPTER EIGHT

ROXANNE did not really expect to hear from Alain again after their angry scene in the park, but, all the same, his silence left a bitter taste in her mouth, for it seemed that the 'unfinished business' to which he had referred had been ended instantly by her declaration that she was involved with someone else.

It would appear that it was all right for *him* to be contemplating remarriage, and at the same time to seek her out in an attempt to have an emotional spring-clean first. She, on the other hand, was supposed to be permanently encased in a time-warp, where she never saw or thought about other men, constantly looking back on her marriage to Alain as the one significant relationship in her life.

He still saw her only as the object of his desire, a desire which, irritatingly, would not go away and leave him to remarry in peace. All he really wanted, she thought angrily, was to make love to her again, to prove that he still possessed that old dominance over her body, and could have her if he chose to. He did not think of her as a person in her own right, with a life of her own that included other relationships.

And in a sense he was right, for what else had she been doing for the last four years but preserving herself, intact and sterile, unable even to think of putting Alain and her disastrous passion for him finally behind her? Other women had bad marriages, got divorced and moved on to find love and happiness with someone else, but she had remained incapable of making that leap.

Because he was still central to her existence, even after four years apart?

This has got to stop, she told herself firmly on the train going back to London. Telling Alain that she had someone else had been an involuntary bid for freedom, a blow struck to recover her pride. It wasn't really true, not in the way she had tried to make him believe. But perhaps she could make it so.

She rang Stuart as soon as she got back to her flat.

'Well, this is an honour,' he said drily. 'Usually I have to leave messages on your machine for three days before you find time to call *me* back!'

'I'm not that bad, surely?' she laughed guiltily. Feeling very forward, she said, 'The thing is, I'm going to be snowed under with work, and then I'll be off to France for the launch, so if you want to take me out to dinner it will have to be tonight.'

'No sooner said than done!' he said promptly. 'I'll phone our favourite restaurant by the river, and I'll pick you up at eight.'

It was all very charmingly organised. He had chosen the table carefully, and there were red roses in a vase. Champagne. Roxanne wore a dress he had not seen before, and went out of her way to be pleasant and amusing company. He was so very nice, thoughtful and considerate, and really deserved better than the occasional crumbs of mild affection she gave him.

He would make a wonderful husband, moreover. There would be no chance of his leaving her alone all the time, or having a fling with someone else. Life with him would be peaceful, pleasant, gracious.

And dull? she could not help asking herself. Well, possibly, but did one have to have a diet of gut-churning excitement, did one need to be forever tossing between the high peaks and the deep, dark troughs? Maybe Alain was right and marriage should be a quieter, less emotional union.

Oh, leave Alain out of it! she told herself crossly, and gave her attention back to the man sitting across the table. He looked so solid and dependable in his neat grey suit, smiling at her, his eyes kind but with a hint of longing in them.

'You seem different tonight,' he told her. 'Maybe I shouldn't push my luck, but I've waited for a long time for the right moment to say this—I'm very, very fond of you, Roxanne. There is nothing I would like better than for you to be my wife. I know you once told me you didn't want to consider marrying again, but I can't help hoping you've had second thoughts about that.'

She smiled gently. Even his proposal was indirect and low-key. She recalled Alain, outside the tourist office with a red rose in his hand, saying, 'I love you. Will you marry me?' with no thought in his head other than that she would say yes. For him, to want was to have. *But not any more.* She was out of his life, and *must* put him finally out of her heart and mind.

'Stuart, I *have* to say this—you know I'm not in love with you,' she said carefully.

He put his hand over hers. It was a comforting feeling, but nothing happened. There was no excitement.

'I'm not asking you to be in love with me—not to begin with, anyhow,' he said earnestly. 'You like me. We get along. I want to make you happy. Isn't it enough for a start? I'm not getting any younger, Roxanne. I should like to be married again, and I'd like best to be married to you. But if you can't...well, I've put my cards on the table. I don't expect an instant answer, but promise me you'll think about it.'

'Yes. Of course,' she said soberly. What he was trying to say was plain enough. As Jeannie had once warned her, and as she had so recently come to realise herself, he would not be satisfied with friendship indefinitely, and it was unfair to keep him dangling. She must decide if she felt able to marry him, and if the answer was no she must leave him free to find someone else.

'My head is full of the launch at the moment,' she excused herself. 'I can't make such an important decision while I'm so involved with that. Can I give you an answer when I come back from France?'

'That's fair enough,' he agreed reasonably, and was it perverse, she wondered, to wish he might have been a little less patient, more importunate? Surely she had had enough of that kind of lordly treatment from Alain? And she really must stop comparing every other man with her ex-husband, setting him up as a standard by which everyone else had to be measured. So long as she continued to do that there would be little chance, ever, of her finding happiness with someone else.

Because she really did not want to spend the rest of her life alone and lonely. The time in France had taught her that, if nothing else. Remembering the closeness she and Alain had shared, in spite of their stormy clashes, she knew that being successful in her career, for all that it meant a lot to her, was not, in itself, enough. She needed the intimate companionship of another human being—no, damn it, she was a woman and she needed to be loved. To love and give in return. Like a butterfly emerging from a long chrysalid sleep, Roxanne stirred tentative wings of hope and feeling. Could she do it?

But it had been no mere excuse to say that beyond the launch she could not think clearly at the moment. Courtney and Weaver was at fever-pitch, last-minute arrangements had to be made to replace those that always mysteriously fell through, and she spent a lot of time

reassuring the anxious executives from Bien Vivre that
it would all come together on the day.

Finally there was a telephone call from France, and
the deep, booming voice of Gaston Burley came through
to her.

'Dear Miss Jefferson, please get out here as soon as
possible!' he begged. 'My wife is constantly at odds with
the caterers about the buffet, journalists keep phoning
us asking questions we cannot answer, and as well as all
this I still have a vineyard to run.'

Roxanne tapped on the top of her desk with her pen.
He was right. Everything that could possibly be done
from this end had been done. Her place, now, was at
Château Burley.

'Don't worry, Monsieur Burley. Everything is going
to be just fine,' she assured him. 'I shall be flying out
just as soon as I can arrange a flight.'

There was always a certain amount of high-tension
nervousness and intense pressure at this stage in a campaign, particularly one as important to the company as
this, but it was a creative stress, a surge of controlled
adrenalin that, ridden properly, was instrumental in
pulling off a successful product launch. But it wasn't
this natural, familiar and entirely necessary 'stage fright'
that had Roxanne chewing at her carefully manicured
nails on the flight out. Rather, it was the prospect of
being back again in France, back in Alain's orbit, and
knowing that he was only a few miles away from her at
any time.

He would know, of course, that she was here. With
his social connections and his family involvement in the
wine trade, he would be well aware of what was taking
place at Château Burley. A good number of influential
local people would be present at the launch, and there
was nothing to prevent him from being among their

number if he so chose. A phone call to Arlette Burley was all that would be needed to get himself invited, and Roxanne shivered, clutching the arms of her seat, trembling at the mere possibility of bumping into him, and unable to say whether she dreaded this or fiercely and secretly desired it.

It was unlikely to happen, she reassured herself. At their last meeting she'd sensed that he had finally washed his hands of her and consigned her firmly to the past after she'd told him that she, too, had someone else. She *had* to hope they would not meet. Oh, but just to catch a glimpse of him from afar, to meet once again those mocking, thoughtful eyes, to feel his tender-sardonic smile resting on her... just the thought of it was enough to send wild emotions racing through her. Emotions she must suppress. No one else would ever excite, arouse, infuriate and fulfil her as Alain once had and still had the ability to, but she had to learn to live without these dangerous and intoxicating sensations.

At Bordeaux Airport was Didier Joly, hopping from one foot to the other in a fine state of strung-out apprehension.

'Thank goodness you are here!' he exclaimed in relief. 'Madame Burley is—how do you say?—having kittens! Furthermore, I am convinced that the weather is going to break! It will ruin everything!'

Roxanne saw clearly that she held the position of linchpin, the still, calm centre around whom the chaotic elements revolved. If she did not remain cool and in command the whole enterprise could lurch towards catastrophe.

'*Soyez tranquille,* Didier,' she urged him, smiling. 'Madame has an attack of nerves, and will be fine once she has another woman to confide in! It is *not* going to rain, and, anyhow, we have a marquee in the event that it does. All will be well.'

She kept repeating this magic formula when she arrived at the château and Arlette virtually collapsed in her arms.

'I cannot cope with this! All these journalists ringing up every minute, and caterers taking over my kitchen!' she wailed. 'Gaston has stamped off down the fields in a temper, declaring that he knows about nothing other than growing grapes and making wine from them! What am I going to do?'

Roxanne put an arm around the tiny woman's shoulders.

'You are going to sit down and have a cup of coffee with me,' she said firmly. 'We have two days to the launch, which gives us plenty of time to sort out all the details. All that Monsieur will have to do is be his charming self and talk about what he knows so very well. I shall deal with the caterers, and answer the journalists' questions—that's why I'm here.'

Strangely enough, beneath her own finely tuned nervousness she was aware of a bedrock of confidence. It would be a success—she had worked with too much dedication for it to be otherwise, and if she had to she would pull the whole thing together with her own hands!

If you can keep your head when all about you
Are losing theirs and blaming it on you . . .

The lines kept running through her head as she applied herself to her various tasks. She could, she *could*. Only one thing could throw her off balance—the appearance, at any point in the proceedings, of Alain Deslandes. Everything else she could manage.

By the time they sat down to dinner that night the Burleys were considerably more relaxed, the buffet difficulties were sorted out, and she had set up a temporary Press office for herself in Gaston's small study. That night she slept in eighteenth-century splendour in a charming rococo bedroom at the château, with windows overlooking the waving green acres. And there, vividly and unexpectedly, she relived in dreams those last, painful days of her life with Alain, the hurt, the disillusionment, and the tragedy.

It was early spring when she had first realised that she had become pregnant, and, as she had told Alain, it had been totally unplanned. She had not even been fully serious herself about having a baby, let alone devious and determined enough to snare him into it.

She could see, at the time, that he did not believe this, and nothing she said convinced him.

'Never mind, *chérie*,' he said wearily at last, impervious to her protests of innocence. 'What's done is done; we are to be parents, and must adapt ourselves to the fact. It's a little soon, but of course I am proud to be the father of our child. So don't cry.'

With that she had to be content. He believed she had sprung this on him to tie him to her more closely, but he forgave her, at least on the surface, and tolerated the *fait accompli*.

Only, from the moment when the pregnancy was confirmed, he seemed to withdraw from her. He never made love to her again, even though she assured him it was perfectly all right to do so, even though she all but begged him to as she grew desperate for the love she felt slipping away from her.

Conversely he became more solicitous, and made every effort to be there, not to leave her alone, and to phone her if at any time he could not avoid being delayed. And, even though she had previously longed for this kind of consideration, now she found herself mourning the old, unpredictable Alain, who would turn up three hours late for dinner, sweep her into his arms and carry her off to bed. There was none of that now. He was sober, polite and punctilious, and she hated it because there was no level on which she could break through to him. She was expecting a baby, her marriage was atrophying from within, and she did not know how, if ever, it could be made right again.

'I am here, am I not? You have what you wanted,' he said coldly one night when she tried to stammer out something of how desolate she felt. 'Sometimes, Roxanne, I think you don't really know what you want, except the opposite of what you have! Please grow up, and stop moving the goal-posts.'

I want the man I fell in love with, she wanted to cry, but it was no use. He hadn't really forgiven her for, as he believed, using her biology to entrap him, and the spontaneous passion they had once shared was a casualty of his mistrust. All she could do was hang on and hope that the birth of the baby would be a fresh start for both of them.

Roxanne remembered exactly how and when she discovered he was seeing someone else. Looking back, it was all so obvious that she wondered how she had not realised it sooner.

To begin with, there were several phone calls to the beach house—a woman's voice, assured, mature and polished.

'A Barbara phoned,' she told him dully when he arrived home. 'She didn't say what it was about.'

'I expect it was Barbara Gilbertin. We are collaborating on a paper,' he replied.

'You never told me that.'

He raised weary, patient brows.

'I cannot be expected to tell you every last little thing I do at work, Roxanne,' he said, discounting at a stroke the many hours he had once spent talking to her about his research.

Barbara rang several times. And then, one afternoon, Alain called Roxanne from Bordeaux to say he would be late.

'We are at a crucial point with this paper,' he said. 'I don't want to break off now. Are you sure you'll be all right?'

It was a Friday evening in July, when the daylight lingered until almost ten. When she had put down the phone Roxanne was seized by a sudden restlessness which would not leave her. She tried to read a book, then switched on the television and switched it off again, and finally wandered aimlessly around the garden. Nothing settled her, and all at once a decision came to her.

Alain had said he would definitely be home tonight—since she had become pregnant he had never left her alone overnight—and she was sure he would take the BAC. They ran regularly into the evening during the summer, and, although she did not know which sailing he would catch, if she went to Royan and waited she could hardly miss him. She could drive there in the little Citroën he had given her, park it, and they could come home together in his car. Perhaps they could stop for dinner at one of the seafront restaurants in St Palais. It would be like old times, and with luck they might . . . just might . . . begin to recapture some of the magic.

Just to act gave her a feeling of renewed hope. She drove into Royan along the coast road, found somewhere to park, and by the time the ferry came in she was standing on the promenade overlooking the terminal, watching its arrival.

Alain was not on board, and she knew it would be an hour before the ferry docked here again. But she didn't mind. Royan was lively in the evenings at this time of year, and she strolled on the beach, listening to a live band playing, glancing around an exhibition of local art, watching a gymkhana—all these activities taking place on the vast sandy beach. When the boat was due to arrive once more she was back in her place to see it nudge slowly into port.

And there was Alain, standing on the top deck. The breeze ruffled his dark hair, and his arms, leaning casually on the rails, were bronzed, his sleeves rolled up to the elbows. He was smiling at her, and her heart knotted up with love for him.

Then she saw that he was *not* smiling at her. In fact, he had not seen her. He was smiling at a woman by his side, a very elegant, attractive woman of about his own age, auburn hair dressed in a smooth topknot, tall, slender frame in an immaculate white sheath dress with a little scarf tied with casual chic around her neck. She had a bulging file of papers under one arm, such as he often carried when he brought work home with him. Roxanne knew, in a blinding flash of intuition, that this had to be Barbara, and that was not all she realised.

She watched them make their way to the car deck together. Alain still had not seen her, and Roxanne noted small details, like the way the woman casually rested her hand on his arm as she eased past him, the look of quiet understanding that passed between them without words.

She did not stay to see more—to do so would have been to admit what she had seen, and it was vital Alain did not know she had been here. To confront him, to force him to admit what was going on, would be the end for them. Turning, she stumbled back to the car park, and switched on her car's engine, desperate to get away.

She made it to the beach house only minutes before his arrival, flung herself into a chair, and tried to appear as if that was where she had spent the entire evening.

He must have given Barbara a lift somewhere, but he made no mention of having had company on the trip, even when she led into the subject by asking casually if the ferry had been busy.

'It always is during the holiday season,' he replied. 'How was your day? Have you been out?'

'Out?' She started guiltily, as if she were the one with something to hide. 'Where should I have been at this time?'

'How should I know? But you have make-up on, and you don't usually wear it to sit around the house,' he observed coolly.

How could she have forgotten something so obvious? And how could she now say casually, 'I came to meet you off the BAC, and who was that woman with you?'?

'I haven't eaten. I thought you might want to go out for a meal,' she invented lamely.

'I only had a snack. We can go if you wish,' he said.

'No...I'm not hungry now. In fact, I feel a little sick,' she excused herself. 'I think I'll go to bed.'

She lay wide awake in the darkness, eyes closed, feigning sleep. When he came to bed, much later, he did not switch on the lamp, but undressed in the dark so as not to disturb her. But there was to be little rest for Roxanne after that. The knowledge was there, lodged painfully inside her, not as a revelation, but as something she must have known, subconsciously, for some time.

No wonder Alain, with his strong sexual drive, had not touched her for so long. No wonder he no longer confided in her, no wonder they only communicated on the most basic level. He had found someone else to fulfil all those needs—that was quite, quite clear. There was nothing to be gained by hoping that the birth of their child would heal the breach between them, for she had already lost him.

In the middle of the night she stirred from a fitful, intermittent doze and came alive to a sharp, piercing pain—an actual physical pain she recognised but had not felt since becoming pregnant, and one she should not be feeling now. Exploring the bedclothes with tentative fingers, she encountered an ominous stickiness, and her sudden scream of fear brought Alain awake instantly.

Sitting up and switching on the light, he said, 'What is it? What's wrong?'

Her face was as pale as white paper, but she could not speak. He pushed back the quilt and saw, at once, the spreading scarlet stain on the sheet beneath her.

'Roxanne!' he exclaimed, and then, 'Don't move,' he ordered her urgently, and she had never seen him move with such lightning swiftness and decision. He was on the phone before she had time to draw breath, then he came back, covered her up and, since there was nothing else either of them could do, held her in his arms until the ambulance arrived.

But Roxanne was already numb with terror and despair. All the time she was aware of the life force oozing out from her. The baby's life, ebbing away, and the last of Alain being stolen from her with it, all her dreams and hopes, all of their love. She scarcely remembered the swift, screeching journey to the hospital at Royan, and the pain-filled minutes mercifully cut off by an anaesthetic-induced oblivion.

When she came round she felt curiously detached from the whole business, as if it had all happened to someone else. She supposed this sensation of floating indifference was the result of the drugs she had been given, which would eventually wear off, but somehow she didn't care.

'I lost the baby, didn't I?' she said woodenly to the doctor, and saw from the expression on his face that she was right.

'Your husband was here all the time. He just went out for some fresh air, and I'm sure he will be back soon,' he said comfortingly.

'I don't want to see him,' she said, and went back to sleep.

The real pain, the pain of loss, only hit her when she awoke again with a clear head. The baby was dead; in fact, had only lived inside her for three short months, but the sense of bereavement was as acute as if she had held her child in her arms and watched it die. She had never dreamed in her worst nightmares that anything could hurt so badly. There was only one thing of which she was quite sure, quite adamant: she did not want to see Alain again. She could not even bear to look at the flowers he had sent her.

For two days she persisted in this refusal, and she knew that the doctors and hospital staff only went along with her wishes and persuaded Alain to do the same because they felt her emotional state was so precarious.

But on the third day he succeeded in overriding them all. She heard him outside her door, saying calmly, levelly, but with absolute determination, 'This has gone on long enough. I must and will see my wife.'

'*Monsieur*—a few minutes only,' she heard the doctor warn him. 'And take great care. I do understand how you feel, but *madame* has been very ill, and is still in a state of shock.'

'I realise that. But she is my *wife*, doctor. And this was my child, too,' Alain reminded him quietly.

Then he was standing at her bedside, and they were alone together. Propped up weakly against her pillows, Roxanne looked at him, and all the emotion she had held inside her for the last two days began to churn and twist, tearing her apart. If she had not seen him on the ferry, if she had not had to face the brutal fact of his betrayal, she was convinced her baby would still be safe inside her. He had killed their child, just as he had killed their love.

'Go away, Alain,' she said dully. 'I don't want to talk to you. I have nothing to say.'

He stared down at her incredulously, his eyes very dark, his face drawn.

'I've spent the best part of two days and two nights pacing that corridor, and you have nothing to say?' he said quietly. 'Do you think I don't know what you have been through? Do you think I haven't suffered with you?'

'You have absolutely no idea of how I feel,' she said in a calm, clear voice. 'It's because of you and that woman of yours—that Barbara—that I'm here. It's because of you that my baby is dead.'

She saw his eyes narrow fractionally, a frown puckering his brow, and she went on quickly, 'Oh, yes, I *know*. I saw you together, so there's no need to pretend.'

'The doctor was right. You are overwrought,' he said decisively. 'I had better ring for the nurse.'

Even now he would not admit it. If he had accepted responsibility for what had happened there might have been a way... but he simply stood there, looking down at her with something like pity. He did not deny his infidelity. How could he? she thought. But his not having the grace to own up to it finally destroyed whatever faith she'd had in him. She could never trust him again, so what was the point?

'Are you leaving now?' she asked bluntly.

'*Bien sûr,* I am leaving,' he said coldly. 'Call me when you have regained your senses. You know the number.'

The next day, against the express wishes of the doctors, Roxanne discharged herself from hospital and left. She wore the only clothes she had, which Alain must have brought in an overnight case and left there for her eventual use.

After phoning the beach house to make sure he was not there at that time, she hired a taxi to take here there, collected her passport, and left before he had a chance to walk in and find her.

In the clothes she stood up in, taking only enough money to pay for her air ticket, Roxanne shook the dust of France from her feet. She had not the remotest intention of ever coming back.

CHAPTER NINE

THE day of the launch was hot, clear and sunny with not a cloud in the sky. Roxanne had the marquee erected all the same—she wasn't prepared to risk having the occasion wrecked by an unexpected shower. The buffet lunch was to be served in the drawing-room anyhow, but she had the long windows all thrown open, and Madame Burley's flagged terrace was set out in the manner of an elegant outdoor café, with little tables under red and white striped umbrellas. The wine-tasting would thus take place out in the sunshine, where the complex, fruity aromas could be savoured at their best under near-perfect conditions.

'It all looks wonderful, my dear,' Arlette praised her unstintingly. 'I am sorry I was in such a state the other day. You have worked so very hard; indeed, you have performed miracles.'

Roxanne demurred smilingly.

'Not really—and *everyone* has worked hard, yourself included,' she said. 'But a launch can be a nerve-racking occasion, I'm well aware.'

'You are obviously a veteran campaigner, in spite of your youth,' Gaston said.

She shook her head.

'Actually, it's the first time I've handled anything on this scale,' she confessed. 'If I'd stopped to think about it I'd have been scared out of my wits. But it's going to be fine now. I can feel it. Your glorious wines, your lovely house, this perfect place—they will do the rest of the hard work for us.'

'We'll drink to that,' Gaston said predictably. 'Why should the journalists have all the fun?'

Then the first of the Press began to arrive, and Roxanne was kept thoroughly busy, greeting, introducing, moving from group to group, always keeping an eye on the waitresses who were serving the wine to ensure that supplies did not run out and that everyone had an opportunity to taste and compare the vintages. In this she was assisted by Bien Vivre's marketing director, who had flown out for the occasion.

'I have to admit that I had my doubts about you in the beginning,' he said as they went in to lunch. 'You seem so young that it didn't seem possible you could have the experience, the authority, to carry this off. But Toby had faith in you, and I trust his judgement. He's not usually wrong, and his faith was more than justified in this instance. I hope you will continue to handle our publicity.'

She blushed with pleasure.

'Why, thank you,' she said. 'I hope so, too. But you'll have to talk to Toby. I'm not sure what plans he has for me.'

'The customer gets what he pays for, Miss Jefferson,' he told her. 'I shall be seeing Toby as soon as I get back to England, and I shall tell him he would be crazy if he moved you from this account now.'

Roxanne sailed through the rest of the day on a swell of quiet satisfaction, wondering only why she didn't feel more euphoric, more fulfilled. She was pleased, of course, that she had done the job, and done it well, but shouldn't she have been positively floating? This day, after all, was the pinnacle of her career achievements so far, and its success meant that all her stated ambitions were now well within her grasp.

So why wasn't she happier? She had everything she wanted—didn't she? She only had to go home and give Stuart an affirmative answer to his proposal and she could have a steady, secure marriage as well as a flourishing career.

But as the afternoon wore on a sense of anticlimax began to creep up on her, and in the deepest corner of her heart she knew why, knew what this brilliant day had lacked. Somehow, despite telling herself that it was unlikely, secretly she had continued to hope that Alain would turn up. If he had only spent five minutes at Château Burley, if he had only smiled at her and wished her well, it would have meant so much to her.

He *had* to know that she was here, and, since he could all too easily have arranged to be present, that meant he had deliberately stayed away. He did not share her errant desire for one last glimpse of the person who had once been the love of his life.

Telling him she had someone else might have boosted her pride, but it had also released him from any lingering obligation to his ex-wife. He felt free of her, finally. She wished she could have said the same.

'You look a little sad,' Arlette said concernedly, appearing at her side as the last of the visitors took their leave. 'You should not, surely. Everything has gone so well.'

Roxanne forced a smile.

'I know it has. I'm probably just suffering from a little tiredness,' she excused herself.

'You are not missing someone special from home, then?' the old lady persisted gently. 'A pretty girl like you must have an admirer?'

Roxanne found this expression rather quaint, almost Edwardian, but somehow it fitted Stuart perfectly. An admirer. She certainly couldn't call him a lover. A fierce wave of desolation swept over her, for which she was utterly unprepared, and she thought bleakly, How could she go home and agree to marry a man she didn't love? It wasn't fair to him. It wasn't fair to herself. There was nothing ahead but loneliness, for all her professional success. The place in her heart which had been Alain's must remain empty.

And then, very strangely, since his name had just been on Roxanne's mind, if unspoken, Arlette said, 'I did invite Alain today as a personal guest. I did not think you would object.'

'But he declined, obviously,' Roxanne said, trying hard to look as if this were of no great consequence to her.

'But no—I never got a reply to my card, which was very odd. Alain is usually meticulously good-mannered,' she said with a small frown.

Just then Didier Joly, who happened to be standing near by, turned. 'That's probably because he isn't well, or so I understand,' he informed her.

Roxanne pivoted, seized by an entirely involuntary anxiety which she could not dismiss, for all she told herself that Alain's health was none of her business. She couldn't help it, because it was so unusual. Alain was never ill. He was almost frantically fit, and during the time she had known him he had never suffered so much as a head cold.

'Not well? What's the matter with him?' she demanded sharply.

Didier looked uncomfortable.

'I...I'm not sure. Some bug or other,' he said. 'It was all rather odd, come to think of it. I phoned him in Bordeaux, but Madame Deslandes took the call. She was quite short—almost abrupt—and obviously did not really want to speak. She told me only that Alain was at La Palmyre, then she hung up on me.'

'Is that all?' Worry was prickling between Roxanne's shoulder-blades. Silly—he's a grown man. Only wives and lovers have the right to such emotions, not ex-wives, she admonished herself, but the nagging anxiety refused to go away.

Didier squirmed under her interrogation.

'Well, almost. I phoned the La Palmyre number yesterday,' he said. 'I was a bit worried, because I can't ever recall Alain's being under the weather. He's there, all right, and he wasn't too pleased at being disturbed. He told me he was not feeling too good, and he was going to take the phone off the hook so he could get some sleep. He said he'd be fine, and I wasn't to worry anyone by telling them,' he added guiltily. 'Now I've done exactly that, and he won't be too pleased if he ever finds out!'

Roxanne tried not to dwell on all of this, but she obviously failed visibly, for Arlette came up to her later, as the staff were clearing away the bottles and glasses, and patted her hand.

'I suppose it's useless my telling you not to worry,' she said. 'Once you have married a man there is a bond you can never really untie, in spite of the divorce papers.'

Roxanne's face was wry.

'It's stupid of me, I know,' she said, 'but would you mind if I tried to phone? He won't thank me, but...I just want to be sure he's all right.'

'My dear, I'd be surprised if you didn't. But if the phone is off the hook you won't get any reply,' she reminded her. 'However, by all means try.'

Roxanne rang the number, but, sure enough, all she got was the unobtainable signal, and by now she really was concerned. What if Alain was seriously ill? The healthiest people had been known to go down with mysterious and threatening ailments, and she pictured him alone there, in pain, or tossing about in delirium.

So he didn't care about her any more—what difference did that make? *She* loved *him*, and that wasn't going to change, no matter what. She knew that now, and, knowing it, couldn't simply stand by and leave him when every instinct was screaming at her that she should be at his side.

Arlette looked at her watch, and then at Roxanne. She must have read her thoughts.

'There's an old shooting-brake in the garage,' she said. 'Take it if you like. If you hurry you can just about catch the next BAC.'

La Palmyre was busy when Roxanne drove through the village centre. It was the hour when people, having come off the beach, were calling in to shops to buy something to cook for their evening meal, or they were going back to their hotels to shower and plan how to spend the evening. There was a determined hedonism in the air, and as she turned down the avenue where the Deslandes beach house was situated she smelled the unmistakable, tempting scent of charcoal as barbecues were lit and their smoke drifted up into the hot, still air.

Alain was here, that was obvious. His car was parked in the drive, although the bungalow was quiet and there was no sign of life. She switched off the engine, hesitating only briefly. Didier had indicated that Alain was here alone, but how could he know? It was possible that Elodie was back in France, and that she was here taking care of him. What could be more natural? Although it would be characteristic of Alain to suffer in silent and dignified isolation.

Roxanne straightened her shoulders. To hell with Elodie, she thought firmly. This was her ex-husband and still, unfortunately for her, the man she loved. There were more important issues than her possible embarrassment, and she had to reassure herself that Alain would be all right.

She tiptoed up the steps to the veranda and tried the door tentatively. It was not locked, and opened easily as she pushed.

There was no one in the *séjour*, and an unearthly quiet was wrapped around the place, permeating the very air. Roxanne's throat was dry with anxiety as she quickly traversed the corridor and quietly opened the door of the room she had once shared with Alain.

He was on the bed, lying flat on his back, one arm outflung, the other bent at the elbow so that his hand shielded his forehead. His eyes were closed, his face drawn, sallow beneath his tan. He looked deeply exhausted.

Without thinking, she ran across the room and sat on the bed by his side. The slight pressure of her weight awoke him; dark grey eyes looked up into her face with slight puzzlement, as if she were a hallucination he expected to disappear into thin air.

'Roxanne?' he said. 'What are you doing here?'

'Does it matter?' she said decisively, resting a hand on his forehead. He felt hot and dry to the touch. 'I'm here, and I'm staying.'

'How did you know?' He managed an irritated frown. 'Didier, I suppose? He can't keep his mouth shut. I was at school with him, and he never could even then.'

'You should be thankful for his indiscretion.' Roxanne reached for his wrist and felt his pulse. She was no nurse, but it felt more or less regular to her, even though he clearly had a raging temperature.

'Well, I'm not. Not at all.' Speech was obviously an effort, but he was perverse, as fiercely independent as ever. 'Go away, Roxanne. You're wasting your time, and I don't need you.'

'You may not need *me* specifically, but you certainly need someone on hand,' she retorted. 'Have you seen a doctor?'

'No, and I don't require one.' He glared at her, anger showing through his discomfort. He plainly hated her seeing him in this state, but she told herself that he would have resisted dependence on anyone just as forcefully. He was sick, and she tried not to take his hostility personally, even though it hurt.

'And why not? You're a medical expert as well now, I suppose,' she said wryly.

'Enough to know what this is—some wretched flu bug that's going around,' he retorted weakly. 'Treatment: rest, aspirin, and being left in peace!'

'Huh,' she said sceptically, ignoring this hint. 'Go right back to sleep, then, and you should be peaceful enough. I'm going to pop down to the shops—but I'll be back.'

'I was afraid of that,' he said in a faint, dry voice, and his eyelids closed even as she watched. The effort of arguing with her had worn him out.

Roxanne slipped quietly but purposefully out, and drove back down to the village centre. She bought fruit, salad, bread, cheese, eggs, mineral water—a whole range of things. She knew Alain wouldn't want anything to eat right now, but once the temperature broke and he felt a little better he was sure to be hungry. She had no intention of leaving until such time.

When she got back to the villa he was still asleep, and she tiptoed quietly into the hall and telephoned Arlette Burley.

'He has the flu,' she said. 'I don't think he should be left alone. I'm going to stick around for a while, but, of course, I still have your car. Is that all right by you?'

'Perfectly,' Arlette said at once. 'You must not worry about the car. And, naturally, you must stay with Alain. The foolish man—but aren't they all like that, so full of silly pride, and so unwilling to seek help?'

Especially from women they'd once loved, but now wanted nothing more to do with, Roxanne thought ruefully.

In the kitchen she chopped up lemons and concocted a drink made from the fruit mixed with water and honey. Taking in the jug and a glass, she placed them on the bedside table.

His eyes fluttered open.

'You still here?' he demanded thickly.

She poured a glass of the lemon drink.

'Sure am. Here—drink this, and don't talk.'

He struggled up on one elbow, peering suspiciously into the glass. 'Not until I know what it is.'

'What, do you think I'm trying to poison you?' she said exasperatedly. Why did men make such impossible invalids? 'It's something my mother used to make when I was ill as a child. Try it—it's good, and you need to replace fluids, anyhow.'

'Oh, very well—if you insist.' He drank two glasses of it appreciatively. 'It *is* good. But there is really no need for you to stay. I don't want you here, acting like a wife.'

'You're sounding better already,' she said acerbically. 'Don't worry. I have no intention of acting like a wife. As soon as you're back on your feet I'll be gone.'

She sensed that he would have liked to put up a more forceful argument but didn't have the strength, and his inability irked him. She watched the lines of his face relax as he drifted off to sleep again, and a strange, sweet triumph stole over her.

He had always been the strong one during their time together, the leader, the teacher, the one to be leaned upon. Maybe the balance would have shifted had they stayed married longer, and as she matured it would have evened out into a more equal relationship. But this was something she had never known, the sweetness of taking care of *him*, of being needed—for he did need her, right now, deny it as he might.

She sat by his side for a long time, watching him, loving him, wishing it could be like this always, a partnership of two adults who succoured and supported and encouraged one another, each providing the strength when the other needed it. The pathos of impossibility wrenched at her heart, the awful knowledge that now, when she had learned what love was truly all about, he did not want her.

At last she crept out, made herself a cup of coffee and a snack, and realised that she was very tired. It had been a full, eventful and exhausting day, and the launch seemed like something that had taken place several lifetimes ago. She felt hot and crumpled in the smart, linen-look dress she had put on that morning and worn throughout this eventful day. Wandering into the spare bedroom, she slipped off her clothes and, wrapping herself in a kimono-type robe she found in the wardrobe, lay down on the bed and closed her eyes.

But she didn't really sleep, only dozed on and off throughout the night, at intervals creeping in to check on Alain. Towards morning he started to toss in his sleep, and she saw he was bathed in a film of perspiration. Alarmed, she fetched a damp flannel and sponged his face, neck and arms. Whether he protested or not, if he was no better by morning she intended calling a doctor.

As she pressed the cool cloth to his hot forehead he moaned suddenly.

'Roxanne!' he called out in such a clear, urgent voice that for a moment she thought him awake, but no, his eyes were still closed. 'Roxanne—you've got it all wrong, you always had! It isn't true!'

She stared down at him. Obviously he was dreaming, and somehow or other she was part of that dream. He seemed so emphatic, so determined to make his point, that she wondered desperately what it was all about. Dreams are mostly nonsense, she told herself, but he sounded so forceful, so full of persuasive logic, that she was gripped by a need to understand exactly what he had been trying to tell her. But he lapsed back into a deep sleep again, and she had to accept that she would never know.

At least, she consoled herself, he was calmer now and had stopped threshing about and sweating. His skin felt cooler to her touch, and thankfully she realised that the illness appeared to be past its worst. Covering him with the quilt, she crept back to her bedroom and snatched a few hours' much needed sleep.

Still only half awake, and without opening her eyes, Roxanne took a deep, instinctive breath of air and knew instantly where she was. She smelled the pines, sharp and resinous, the tang of the ocean, clean and salty, and she had woken here too many times not to know, even before she was fully conscious, that she was at La Palmyre.

She got out of bed and opened the shutters, and the bright, clear sunlight invaded the room, eager after being shut out for so long. Glancing at her watch, she saw that it was after ten-thirty. She had slept late after her disturbed night... Alain! She gasped, and hurried along the corridor to his bedroom.

He was lying back against the pillows, but wide awake, and with eyes that were alert and clear once more as they sought hers. Although he still looked a little drained, there was no doubt that this was the Alain she knew, in full possession of all his senses if, as yet, not quite his full strength.

'You look much better!' she said delightedly.

'I feel much better.' He smiled gravely. 'I suppose it had to be you last night, doing the Florence Nightingale bit with the cold compress?'

'You remember that?' she said, surprised.

'Only vaguely. Why? Are there bits I can't remember that were more interesting? I suppose not—I was in no fit state.' A ghost of the Boy Scout grin creased his mouth, and Roxanne found herself blushing.

'You're impossible!' she remonstrated. 'You always were!'

'I'm impossibly sweaty and filthy, of that I'm sure,' he said cheerfully, sitting up and swinging his legs out of bed. 'I'm going to have a shower, right this minute.'

'Are you sure? You mustn't overtax your strength too soon——' she began anxiously, and he stood up.

'Look—no hands! Roxanne, I stink, and I'm going to clean up. Are you volunteering to scrub my back?'

'Certainly not!' she cried, flustered. Alain, ill and immobile in bed, was one thing. Alain, up and about, testing her wits every minute, was quite another.

'There are no advantages to being an invalid these days,' he grinned at her over his shoulder.

She watched him disappear down the corridor, and gave a wry shake of the head. Without him, life was all monochrome—he was colour and excitement and motion. How had she lived without him for so long? How was she going to learn to do so all over again?

'Are you hungry?' she called after him.

His head reappeared briefly round the door of the *salle d'eau*.

'I am in imminent danger of starvation,' he replied quite seriously.

Roxanne hummed to herself as she put brioches in the oven to warm, and coffee on to percolate. She opened the doors on to the veranda and laid the small table out there, happily fetching jam and honey, yoghurt and a bowl of fresh fruit. The sun was shining, the coffee smelled delicious, and Alain was well again. She didn't want to think about anything beyond today.

But, of course, that reminded her instantly, and she clapped a hand to her mouth. She should not be here, even now. She should be on her way back to England.

From the hall she heard water still splashing in the shower as she picked up the phone and dialled Courtney and Weaver's number.

'Roxanne! We were all wondering what had happened to you,' Toby's secretary exclaimed. 'You're missing all the fun. Toby's in a meeting with Mike Palmer from Bien Vivre at this very minute, and I think they're singing your praises. Would this be an appropriate moment to put you through?'

'No, don't do that,' Roxanne said quickly. 'Just give him a message. Tell him that I'm still in France, that something personal has cropped up and I have to take a day or so of my leave.'

'But he's yelling for you! When will you be in?' the secretary wailed.

'As soon as possible,' Roxanne said evasively, and rang off before she was obliged to answer any more questions.

She turned just as Alain emerged from the shower-room. He wore nothing more than a towel knotted around his waist, the clean, tanned skin of his torso still glistening with drops of water, his hair wet and dark. Roxanne was suddenly reminded that she, too, was scantily dressed; she was still wearing only the thin robe, with nothing underneath.

A sudden charge of electricity rippled the quiet atmosphere. This was dangerous. She knew this man intimately, had once lived with him as his wife, and only weeks ago, here in this very house, she had very nearly allowed him to make love to her.

They stood still, looking at one another for a long moment, and she knew with absolute certainty that if he touched her now there was no power in heaven or on earth that could prevent nature's taking its course. They would make love. Her stomach tightened; she tingled all over, waiting for that one, fatal move which would take them irrevocably over the brink.

Then he said briskly, 'I'm going to get dressed, and I think it would be a good idea if you did the same. If you hunt in the drawers of the spare bedroom you'll find one or two things of yours which got left behind when I sent your clothes on to you.'

Dismissed, but still shaken, she did as he bade her, and found, among other things, a pair of shorts and a

cotton sun-top—so skimpy that she couldn't wear a bra
under it—with thin shoestring straps. She pulled them
on with hands that trembled, and, looking in the mirror,
saw briefly the girl she had once been, wearing clothes
which had once belonged to that girl. Cheap and cheerful
things she had brought with her from England, before
she had become Madame Alain Deslandes, and long,
long before her metamorphosis into Roxanne Jefferson,
public-relations executive.

Alain was already on the veranda, tucking into the
brioches, and he eyed her oddly as she emerged, as if
the sight of her took him, too, back to the time when
he had loved that girl.

'It's a bit like pretending to be someone else,' she said
with an uneasy little laugh. 'It isn't really me any more.'

'Yes. It does stretch credulity a little,' he agreed. 'To
think that once——' He stopped, quite deliberately, and
then continued in a different vein. 'I should thank you
for last night. I *do* thank you.'

'*De rien,*' she said, shrugging casually. 'But whatever
made you come here, all alone, if you weren't well? You
would have been more comfortable and well looked after
at home.'

'My parents' home, you mean?' he said, and she
thought he sounded a little strained. 'I didn't know I
was going to be ill. This flu comes on very suddenly. I
was fine when I arrived here.'

'Perhaps you should go back to convalesce,' she suggested. 'You look much better, but a bad bout of flu
can be debilitating.. I'll drive you if you like. It would
be less tiring for you.'

'No!' he exclaimed sharply. There was a short hesitation, and then he said, 'You're being very noble, so
perhaps I had better tell you...I had a...a difference

of opinion with my mother. I think it is probably best that I stay here.'

'I thought you could do no wrong in your mother's eyes,' she said flippantly, but his face now wore that closed expression which meant she would get no more out of him, however hard she tried. All the same, she couldn't resist adding slyly, 'The only thing you ever did that displeased her was marry me, and, since I'm given to understand she absolutely adores Elodie, your impending nuptials can't be the problem.'

'Since you will never know, you shouldn't over-tire your imagination unduly,' he said with a flash of dry anger.

'I won't!' she said, stung, and picked up the coffee-pot to refill it. 'I can assure you, I'm not *that* interested in any aspect of your life!'

'So why are you here, Roxanne?' he asked challengingly. 'Why did you come charging over here in a borrowed car if you are so supremely uninterested? Was the launch less of a triumph than you would have liked it to be?'

'On the contrary, the launch went off very well indeed,' she retorted. 'I came because you were ill and alone, and I haven't broken the habit of worrying about you! That's all there is to it.'

'Really?' His eyes were lazy, but intent. '*Eh bien*, now I'm well again, so what's keeping you? You can stop worrying and go back to your wonderful job, and your marvellous new lover.'

Roxanne averted her gaze, afraid that her eyes would tell him what she could not, that she had never had, or ever wanted, any other lover but him. Nor could she tell him how desperately important it had become that he did not send her away, not now, not at once... so that she could have, if nothing else, the rest of this day with him.

'It might not have occurred to you, but I am rather tired,' she said. 'The Florence Nightingale bit kept me up much of the night, and I'd like to recoup my energies before I face the horrors of international travel.'

He shrugged.

'*D'accord.* As you wish,' he said nonchalantly, and she breathed again. It was useless to remind herself that she had to go, if not now then very soon. Equally useless to ask why she was prolonging the agony.

She had come back to France insistent that she hated him for what he had done to her all those years ago. But she didn't—not any more. It was the old, immature Roxanne who had clung so tightly to those bitter, resentful feelings, and even then perhaps they had been no more than a shield against her pain. Not daring to admit that she still loved him regardless, she had turned that love inside out and called it hatred.

But every time she saw him, even though they fought— she and Alain would find *something* to argue about in the Garden of Eden, she thought wryly—every time they met she understood more and more of the man she loved, simply because she herself had grown, had matured emotionally.

Last night, as she'd sat by his side watching him toss feverishly, she'd admitted to herself that nothing was as cut and dried as her youthful counterpart had believed. Right, wrong; guilty, innocent; black, white—life, for the most part, was not so neatly and conveniently divided.

He had turned to another woman, it was true, but she must bear at least some of the blame for that. Her blinkered possessiveness must have been hard to live with, and when he'd thought she had deliberately become pregnant against his wishes maybe that had been the last straw. There had undoubtedly been faults on both sides, but if she hadn't taken off so precipitately there might have been a chance of saving their marriage. She had refused to give it that chance.

There was no point, now, in rehashing the past and telling him all this. He had lost whatever interest he might once have had in her reasons and motives. He had Elodie now, and, whatever disagreement he might have had with his mother, they would be reconciled by the marriage Madame Deslandes so strongly desired. And Alain believed that she, Roxanne, had someone else. Happy endings all round!

Only Roxanne knew that her first duty on her return to England would be to put Stuart out of his misery. Marrying a man you didn't love was a gamble. Marrying him when you were still in love with someone else was lunacy.

But all that was in the future, and she would face it when she came to it. For now she had today, and she would stretch out every minute, making each one count as a lifetime. The lifetime with Alain that she had once foolishly thrown away, and could never regain, compressed into a single day.

Breakfast had been so late that neither of them was hungry at lunchtime, and they spent most of the afternoon in the garden, stretched out on the grass. From time to time Alain slept, and she didn't disturb him, convinced that this was the best way for him to restore his usual healthy metabolism. When he was awake they talked, but only lightly, casually, touching on nothing of great importance, nothing that involved either of their lives beyond this day.

On her part this was quite deliberate. She didn't want to think about the grey future which did not include him, let alone discuss it. Why he went along with this tacit conspiracy she could not have said. The kindest explanation was that he, too, was suffering from a brief bout of nostalgia, but it could have been simply that he couldn't be bothered, and wasn't really concerned whether she was here or not.

Late in the afternoon he looked at his watch and said, 'I think I'll take a stroll down to the newsagent's and see if they still have a copy of *Le Monde*.'

'No—you rest. I'll go,' she said quickly. 'I want to go to the shops, anyhow.'

He lay back, regarding her with wry curiosity.

'If you insist. But it's a little too late for all this wifely concern,' he observed.

This was a dangerous line of conversation which she thought it best to avoid, so she promptly made herself scarce.

Her trip to the shops included, in addition to his newspaper, two large, thick steaks and a litre of good red wine, and on her return she rummaged in the garden shed where the charcoal was kept, and set about lighting the barbecue.

'Playing at house, are you?' he demanded lightly, but there was a warning undertone to his voice, and Roxanne gave a casual shrug.

'We have to eat,' she said briskly, 'and it seems a shame to be indoors when it's so warm. Keep an eye on the coals, will you, while I go and make a salad?'

So what if she was playing at house? she asked herself as she shredded lettuce and chopped tomatoes. Was she also playing at being something she was not, and had not been in years... Alain's wife? Could it harm? By tomorrow she would be gone, she promised. He would be free of her once and for all.

But when she emerged from the kitchen in order to lay the terrace table she found to her surprise that he had entered into the spirit of the thing. The wine was de-corked to breathe, and he was turning the coals on the barbecue to encourage them to glow.

'Pass the steaks,' he ordered, smiling faintly. 'I never met a woman yet who was any good at barbecuing.'

The tantalising aroma of charcoal drifting in the air, the sizzle of meat making contact with the hot grid, the cool shade of the pines all around, and the warmth of the sun high above them—all this was part of the remembered fabric of the life they had once shared and discarded. There were other, more painful memories, but Roxanne found that they had all left her now, and in this poignant moment she recalled only what was good.

Alain stood beside her, pouring wine into her glass, and the sun's rays, slanting through the trees, obscured his expression as she looked up at him. For a breathless split-second she thought he was going to bend his head and touch her mouth with his, and she inhaled sharply with anticipation. But if he'd had any such intention he did not follow it through.

'Come and eat,' he said. 'The steaks will be ready now.'

'Surely not? Why do you French like your meat with the blood running out?' She covered up her emotional dismay with an attempt at flippant humour.

'For much the same reason as you English like yours charred to a frazzle.' He raised his glass, and, although the sun was still in her eyes, she knew he was smiling. *'Vive la différence. Vive l'entente cordiale,'* he said drily.

They sat for a long time after they had eaten, drinking the wine and watching a red sunset stain the sky. They did not speak—there was no need, for now, as ever before, they had perfect companionship, a rapport so complete that it all but enveloped them. Why now? she thought sadly. Why now, when it's all ending?

His hand lay alongside hers on the table, so close that they were almost touching, and she longed to reach out and feel her fingers enclosed in his warm clasp. As if her thoughts had touched him he turned towards her, his eyes suddenly very sober and thoughtful.

'Roxanne——'

She leapt up promptly.

'I have to wash the dishes——'

'Leave them,' he said quietly and with a strength of authority that rooted her to the spot. 'Roxanne—this has to stop. Right now. It isn't good for either of us.'

She had seen this coming all day, and had carefully avoided it, but now she could no longer put off the awful moment, or deter him from enforcing it.

'I—I don't know what you mean,' she stammered clumsily.

'Yes, you do, all too well,' he contradicted implacably. 'All this is very nice, but it's play-acting, isn't it? Well, the play is over. It's getting late, and you can't stop here tonight.'

'I was here last night,' she argued. 'We're grown-up people. It's no big deal.'

'Last night was different, and you know it,' he said firmly. 'You could have come into my room stark naked and I couldn't have done much about it. But if you sleep under this roof tonight you know—we *both* know what will happen.'

'That's ridiculous, Alain!' Roxanne felt uncomfortably hot and flustered, her heart thumping alarmingly, her throat dry and tight. 'Because you have this insane and rather insulting notion that we shan't be able to restrain ourselves you want me to drive back to Château Burley now! It's too late even to catch the BAC.'

'I wouldn't dream of suggesting it, especially after you've just helped me to dispose of a bottle of wine,' he said reproachfully. 'All I said was that you should not stay here. Get changed and get your things together. I'll phone up and book you into the Palmyrotel.'

She knew he meant it, and what was more she knew that he was right, and yet she didn't want to go. She didn't want to leave him tonight or ever. But one look at his face, hard, set, as if graven in stone, told her that it was useless to plead. It was the terrible awareness that—desire her as he might—he didn't *want* to be intimately and sexually involved with her again that caused her resistance to collapse all at once.

'All right,' she said wearily. 'Give me five minutes.'

She turned abruptly, blindly, because she was starting to cry, and was desperate he should not know it, and, blundering her way across the dimly lit terrace, she stumbled into the wooden framework of the open French door, bumping her head. The sudden pain, compounding her distress, made her let out an agonised and involuntary howl.

'Oh, damn—damn!' she swore furiously.

He was across the terrace in an instant, pushing aside a chair to get to her, his arms closing protectively around her.

'Roxanne—*chérie*—you're hurt...let me see,' he urged her gently.

'I banged my head—it's nothing,' she muttered, struggling in his arms, trying to free herself, but he wouldn't let go of her. 'Alain, let me go! Let me go this minute!' she begged furiously, lifting her angry, tear-streaked face to his.

'You're crying,' he said, touching her cheek with his fingers. 'Did it hurt that much?'

'No, it did *not*!' she exclaimed exasperatedly. How could such a clever man be so obtuse? 'Just let me go—please!'

She had fought all day to stay—now she only wanted to run like a frightened chicken because she couldn't cope with the searing emotions that were tugging at her, the pain she knew would be the end result if he held her any longer in his arms. But he didn't release her. One moment they were glaring at one another like adversaries, the next, his mouth was on hers, dragging her soul from her body, drowning her in sweetness.

The contact was fatal, just as he had warned her it would be, as she must have known too if she'd had an ounce of sense. His hands closed at her waist, slid down to her hips, moulding her body to his, her arms slipped around his neck, and the kiss went on and on, to the point where she thought she must surely explode.

'You see?' he said roughly when at last he allowed her to breathe again, only to lift her up bodily in his arms. 'I told you, didn't I? I want you, Roxanne—and I have to have you right now.'

'I want you, too,' she said recklessly, knowing now that they were on a roller-coaster of passion that could not be stopped.

Kicking open the doors, he carried her into his half-shuttered bedroom, and they reached the bed just in time, her fingers swiftly unbuttoning his shirt, his releasing the straps of her sun-top.

Tomorrow she was going to regret this, Roxanne thought hazily, but tonight she was past caring. Tonight there was only the sweet splendour of their naked bodies close together, hands and lips touching, limbs entwined. And at last the glory she had never forgotten, and had needed for so long—the wonder of him inside her, two as one, as it was meant to be. With a sharp cry, half triumph, half surrender, she gave him back what had, in reality, been his all along.

CHAPTER TEN

SOME things don't change, Roxanne thought, lying beside her still sleeping ex-husband, and this was one of them. He was still the same splendid and exacting lover he had been four years ago, and she had responded to him as fully, as delightedly, now as she had then.

On the brink of sleep, he had murmured into her hair, 'That should not have happened—but I knew it would, and I'm not apologising for it.'

'I wouldn't have expected you to,' she had replied lazily, leaning her head on his shoulder. 'Perhaps we had to be lovers again, Alain—to rid our respective systems of one another. Now we can...we can forget.'

Or you can, she thought. Her last, most valuable gift to him—his freedom. For this time, when she went away, she would not be back. Not for Courtney and Weaver or Bien Vivre, even if it cost her her career. Not for a king's ransom. There was nothing worth the anguish of risking meeting Alain, married to someone else. The man she would always think of as *her* husband, *her* love.

The things lovers said to each other in the dark privacy of night were tender and often nonsensical, but they were right at the time. He had told her she was beautiful, more beautiful than she had been four years ago, and demanded of her, even as he'd carried her over the edge of ecstasy, if anyone else had ever made her feel like this. No one, she had cried out truthfully, no one, and no one ever would. She had given herself without restraint, and even now, watching the daylight creep under the shutters, she didn't really wish it had been otherwise.

But what she did not want was a post-mortem. She had rather it ended here, with the good memories of the night, before they had a chance to wound one another again, and before she had to think too hard about Elodie, or keep up a smiling pretence about her involvement with Stuart.

Roxanne stole a last look at Alain's face, oddly defenceless in sleep, and slipped quietly out from the curve of his arm without disturbing him. Tiptoeing into the spare bedroom, she dressed quickly in the linen-look dress she had arrived in, pushed her feet into her shoes and picked up her handbag.

Pausing in the *séjour*, she found a pen and wrote on a scrap of paper, *'Au revoir,* Alain. Be happy. Roxanne,' and then crept out of the house, closing the door quietly behind her.

La Palmyre was just stirring as she drove through the centre. Two men walking dogs stopped for a chat. A woman cycled past, deftly balancing a long baguette under her arm. The sun sparkled on the white paint and black masts of the boats bobbing in the small marina, and beyond it the Atlantic Ocean rolled silkily in across the clean pale golden sweep of the shore.

Roxanne turned her eyes resolutely from this endearing scene, said goodbye to it in her heart and concentrated on the road ahead.

Gaston and Arlette were just finishing breakfast when she turned up at Château Burley. Like most people of their age, they did not sleep late, and moreover had a vineyard to keep them busy from dawn to dusk, but they were astonished to see Roxanne so early.

'I'm sorry to disturb you,' she apologised, 'but I had to bring back your car and collect the rest of my luggage. If I may just ring the airport to find out about flights, and get a cab to take me there...?'

Arlette would not hear of Roxanne's ordering a taxi. One of the estate workers would drive her to the airport, she insisted.

'But you must tell us—how is poor Alain?' she asked worriedly.

'He did have a nasty bout of summer flu, but he's much better. He'll be fine now,' Roxanne reassured her. That was really all she wanted to say on the subject of Alain to this discerning old lady, but Arlette clucked her tongue regretfully.

'I always had the feeling that there was a lot left between the two of you,' she said. 'He cared a lot for you, you know. I thought that perhaps you might get back together.'

Roxanne shook her head emphatically.

'He cares a lot for someone else now,' she said, trying not to think about the passionate night they had spent together.

'Oh, I suppose you mean that young woman with the fashion shop,' Arlette sniffed dismissively. 'He's not in love with her, my dear, even if Deslandes *mère* thinks she's the pussycat's pyjamas!'

Roxanne had to smile, if a trifle wistfully, at this terminology.

'I thought that was the way things were done in such families over here,' she said wryly.

'It wasn't the way Gaston and I did it,' Arlette said firmly. 'I married him after a three-day courtship before he went off to fight with the Free French...it was during the War. My father threatened to have his hide, but I believed, and still believe, that you have to make a stand for what you want! Although to look at the love of my life now, skulking behind his newspaper, you wouldn't think he had a scrap of romance in him!'

Roxanne caught the twinkle in Gaston's bright blue eyes as they met his wife's, and didn't believe a word of that. How she wished she could live with Alain long enough to reach the safe harbour that sheltered this sprightly and still loving couple.

Unfortunately that wasn't what Alain wanted, she thought.

'It's not like that between us,' she said hastily. 'We loved each other once, but things didn't work out, and...that's all there is to it.'

She couldn't get a flight to London until late that afternoon, and the thought of sitting around the airport all day, succumbing to ever deeper gloom and misery, appalled her. She had crested through last night on an unthinking wave of passion, had held herself together long enough to allow her to walk out of Alain's life, as she was convinced he wanted her to do, but now the idea of several hours of miserable inaction was too much for her.

On a sudden, crazy impulse, having checked in her luggage, she hired a taxi to take her into Bordeaux. The last part of Alain she could have, for an hour or two, was his city. That was the only way she could feel close to him now, and if she was never to see either of them again perhaps it was something she had to do.

Opposite the Girondin Monument, she stood for a while watching the wheeling traffic, the buzz of human activity, and the gulls circling noisily in the blue sky overhead, and then, slowly savouring each poignant moment, she walked up the Cours du Trente-Juillet, retracing her steps instinctively towards the Office de Tourisme.

And then her heart stopped, literally, and remained suspended, and she was breathless for a moment, as across the road she saw a tall, upright, quickly striding figure emerge from that building and mingle with the crowd. The dark, neatly cropped head, the firm, determined shoulders, the purposeful walk—it could not possibly be Alain, whom she had left sleeping in La Palmyre several hours ago! Could it?

The lights changed, and two lanes of traffic hurtled past, immobilising her on the pavement. Her heartbeat thumped painfully as she strained her eyes, searching for that illusion among the crowd. It couldn't be! She looked at her watch and reasoned that yes, it just might.

So what? her reasoning mind might have asked. Leave him free to go about his life, as you intended. But Roxanne had abandoned reason. She raced across the road, almost before the red light indicated that it was safe to do so, cars honking furiously at her as she dodged them.

It had to be Alain—she couldn't be mistaken about someone she knew so intimately—and she had to catch up with him. Why? To tell him what she should have told him before she'd sneaked out of his bed like a thief. That it took two to make a marriage, and two to break one up, and she had been as involved as he in the process. That she no longer blamed him for the loss of her unborn baby. These things happened, and who knew what had really caused her to miscarry? It was wrong of her to hang that burden around his neck forever.

Most of all she wanted to wish him well—sincerely and from the bottom of her heart. To say 'better luck next time', because she truly loved him and didn't want

him to embark on a new marriage with an old, failed
relationship shadowing him like an albatross.

She reached the opposite side of the road, but there
was no sign of him anywhere—if, indeed, it had been
Alain, and not a figment of her wishful imagination.
Roxanne could very easily have wept, standing there on
the busy pavement.

But she didn't. You have to make a stand for what
you want, Arlette Burley had said. Roxanne didn't want
to leave Alain at all, but, since she could not have what
she wanted, she would settle for doing the right thing,
as she saw it. She walked determinedly into the tourist
office.

The girl on the desk was a stranger to her, of course,
but Roxanne smiled at her.

'*Bonjour, mademoiselle,*' she said. 'Tell me—are you
acquainted with Monsieur Alain Deslandes?'

The girl looked surprised, but she smiled in return.

'*Bien sûr,*' she said. 'That is to say, I know him by
sight.'

Roxanne drew a deep breath.

'Was he here a minute or two ago?'

'Why, yes, *mademoiselle*, he was, although for what
purpose I don't know. He came in, then changed his
mind and went straight out again.'

Roxanne whirled, and, calling, '*Merci!*' over her
shoulder, dashed out into the street again. It *was* Alain
she had seen! She had not been mistaken. But where had
he gone? Where was he heading?

She had reached the intersection with the Rue
Ste-Catherine before the utter futility of her search hit
her like the blast from a bomb. How could she possibly
hope to find one man in a city this size? He could be
virtually anywhere. Even if she assumed he had headed

in this direction, the old city was a maze of interconnecting streets and squares. He could have turned off down any one of these narrow alleys, could be in any one of a thousand cafés or bookshops, or...who knew? He might have made an appointment to meet someone...possibly even Elodie.

Roxanne pictured him waking up in La Palmyre and finding her gone. Shrugging his shoulders nonchalantly...ah, well, that was that. The girl he had once married had been good for a night of reminiscent passion, but now she had gone it was time to get on with his life. She imagined him sitting up in bed, one bronzed arm reaching out, the hand closing over the telephone receiver...

She couldn't take any more. The busy pedestrianised street, the fine old buildings, the shops and cafés, all merged into a whirling kaleidoscope, spinning around her head. She had lost him once, found him, and lost him yet again, and it was more than she could bear. Roxanne staggered to a pavement café and collapsed on to a chair, her elbows on the table, head buried in her hands. Tears began to trickle down her cheeks, and she didn't care that people might be watching her. What did it matter? Her life had no meaning; it was empty and barren and pointless.

Someone had stopped at her table, she was dimly aware, because their shade blocked the sun. The waiter, she supposed, but she was too distraught to raise her head, let alone speak. Then there was the brisk scraping of a chair, and two warm, strong hands closed over hers.

'*Qu'est-ce que tu as?*' Alain's voice spoke to her gently in French, the language they had always spoken in intimacy. 'What's wrong? Don't cry, *petite*, please—I can't bear to see you cry.'

Roxanne lifted her tearful face just a little, and found that this miracle was no delusion. It *was* Alain sitting beside her, his eyes looking into hers, full of tender concern, his hands holding hers.

She sniffed, gulped. 'I was looking for you!' she muttered foolishly.

'And now you have found me. Or, rather, I found you,' he said. 'I was looking for you, too, and it would seem I made a better job of it.'

He summoned a waiter.

'Coffee, please—two,' he ordered quietly. Producing a clean tissue from his pocket, he dabbed at her face. 'There. It's a good thing you are not wearing make-up. But I suppose you didn't have time to put it on,' he said, smiling pointedly. 'Did you really think you could steal away from me like that, without explanations? *Vilaine!*'

His voice was stern but gentle at the same time, and Roxanne, overcome by the sheer magic of his being there when she had thought him lost forever, managed only to stutter, 'B-but how——?'

'How did I catch up with you?' He laughed. 'It was not too difficult. I phoned Château Burley, knowing you would have to return their car, and Arlette told me you had just left for the airport. So I headed straight there. I narrowly missed you there, too, but someone recalled a girl answering your description calling a cab. Where else would you have come but here? I drove very fast— illegally so. I know you, Roxanne—very well,' he added in a low voice which throbbed with emotion stronger than she'd ever recalled his revealing so readily before. 'I knew which route you would take, because I would have done the same thing myself. But if I had not found you here I would have gone back to the airport and waited until you turned up for your flight.'

She was looking directly into his eyes now, and the busy street, the tables all around, receded into the distance, leaving them isolated in a little concentrated moment of living, where there could no longer be deceit or pretence, but only the essential truth that mattered.

'Why?' she whispered urgently. '*Why* did you follow me...track me down? What do you want of me, Alain?'

The waiter set the coffee on the table in front of them, unheeded, and then made himself scarce, sensing that these two had eyes and thoughts only for each other.

'I want you to marry me,' Alain said clearly. 'I want your answer, here and now, in words of one syllable and without hesitation. Yes or no.'

The last of the mists cleared from her mind, the beat of her heart settled to a proper rhythm, and she saw, without any difficulty, the only path she could take, no matter what problems following it would involve. Her fingers tightened over his, and her smile was heartrendingly lovely, had she but known it.

'Yes,' she said, promptly and clearly, not a hint of equivocation in her voice. 'Yes, I'll marry you. Whenever you like.'

Had any of his students been watching they would have been astounded to see their calm, reserved, somewhat awe-inspiring history lecturer leap to his feet, pull the blonde young woman into his arms and whirl her around in the air, before clasping her firmly to him. Several of the café patrons looked up at this scene in mild amazement, not showing too much alarm because they were sophisticated Bordelais, after all, and this was obviously nothing more than a severe case of *l'amour*.

'She said yes!' he announced delightedly, and there was a round of good-natured applause.

'I must be mad!' Roxanne added, but she kept her arms tightly around Alain.

He slung a handful of coins on the table to pay for the coffee. It was cold, anyhow.

'Let's get out of here,' he muttered, grinning, 'before they decide we're both mad!'

Arms entwined, they walked down the street and he led her along a narrow alley which branched off into a small, quiet square. Here, with only busily pecking pigeons as an audience, he drew her down beside him on a bench beneath a shady tree, and kissed her until she was dizzy with happiness. When at last he released her mouth he still held both of her hands in a firm grip.

'Did you really think, after last night, that I would ever let you go?' he demanded. 'Do you think we could still feel like that, and *not* be together?'

Still glowing, but coming slowly back to earth, she said, 'We felt like that once before, but it didn't help us. I thought you only wanted to make love to me—to get me out of your system.'

'Was that what *you* wanted?' he persisted, and she shook her head.

'No...but there was Elodie, and I thought you had decided that *she* was the right one for you.'

'I told Elodie, before you came back, that I couldn't consider marriage after all,' he said. 'I explained to her that it would not be fair to either of us. Better that I should remain single if I could not have you. I told my parents that, too.'

She caught her breath, and he nodded.

'Yes, that was the cause of the disagreement with my mother. I told her that I was still in love with you, and that she would simply have to understand that it was you or no one.'

Roxanne groaned.

'Oh, no, Alain—once again I'm going to come between you and your family!' she exclaimed sadly.

'No, my love, you are not. My mother accepted what I said after a talk with my father. I think he understands, and he will help her to get used to the idea. But it seemed better to move out and let her calm down. She'll come round to it, you'll see. Not that it would have made a scrap of difference to me had she not.'

He drew her even closer.

'That's why I had to ask you first—to be sure that you still loved me enough, in spite of everything, to come back to me. I tried to send you away, to be fair to your Stuart, but it didn't work. My family, Elodie, Stuart— what we felt for each other had to be more important than any of them.'

'I had already decided I could not marry Stuart,' Roxanne said. 'There was never any real emotional involvement on my part, you see. I only wanted you to think there was. We were never lovers.' She took a deep breath. '*You* are the only lover I have ever had.'

His eyes darkened, but this time with delight, not anger.

'Is this true?'

'I swear it,' she said solemnly. 'I wanted to find you today to tell you that I no longer blamed you solely for the break-up. I even understand, now, why you turned to that Barbara——'

She thought his hands would crush her as he said impatiently, 'Roxanne, you surely do not still believe that— if you ever did? There was never anything between Barbara Gilbertin and myself but friendship and a partnership of colleagues. She's married to an Australian now, and lives in Perth.'

She stared at him, not understanding, but quite, quite sure that what he was telling her now was the absolute truth.

'But of course I believed it!' she said. 'It was why I left you. Why didn't you explain this to me at the time?'

'Because I was a proud, stiff-necked idiot!' he said with a rueful shrug. 'But be honest, *ma chérie*, would you have believed me? You were so convinced of your own rightness, and I did not see why I should defend myself and prove anything—you either trusted me or you did not. Besides, by then I thought you had realised you had made a mistake in marrying me, and wanted only a quick way out. You were so young, and I had expected you to adapt too quickly. I'd made few allowances, and it seemed the only honourable thing to do was to give you the excuse you needed. To let you go, to be free to start again.'

She rested her head on his shoulder.

'I loved you so much,' she confessed. 'I thought you didn't want me any more, but I wasn't going to beg for your love.'

'Like hell!' he groaned. 'I was obsessed with you, but I was angry when I thought you had deliberately become pregnant against my wishes.'

'No.' Her protest was quiet but vehement. 'I didn't. That you *must* believe. I was naïve and immature and possessive, but I would not have stooped to that.'

Her face was so intense, so concerned, that he bent and kissed her again.

'I know that now, my love. But I never stopped loving you—I went to America chiefly to get away from the memories of you that were all around me here. When I came back not only were they still present, everywhere, but you came back in person.'

'Reluctantly, and in fear and trembling, for the same reasons,' she said, a smile lighting her face. 'I tried to hate you, but I couldn't keep it up, although every time we met we struck sparks off one another.'

'We probably always will,' he laughed softly. 'It will never be a quiet relationship, and why should we want it to be? At least we will never bore one another! But we *have* changed, Roxanne, sufficiently to understand one another far better. I love the woman you are now even more than I loved the girl you once were. I'll never allow you to escape from me again.'

'You won't have to. I've learned my lesson, and I love you far too much now to try,' she promised. Her eyes began to sparkle wickedly. 'Alain, take me back to La Palmyre today. Now. I want to be alone with you. Let's have the honeymoon before the wedding!'

The sinful gleam in his eyes more than matched hers as he drew her to her feet and folded her into his arms.

'By all means, my insatiable darling,' he said softly. 'But what makes you think it's going to end then?'

The bells in the old city were chiming the hour as they walked slowly along the street, arms around each other's waists, and overhead gulls and swallows wheeled in celebration. Roxanne rested her head against the shoulder of the man she loved, and a contented smile creased her lips. She had come home.

HARLEQUIN ROMANCE®

**Harlequin Romance
has love in
store for you!**

Don't miss next
month's title in

THE BRIDAL COLLECTION

A WHOLESALE ARRANGEMENT
by Day Leclaire

THE BRIDE *needed* the Groom.
THE GROOM *wanted* the Bride.
BUT THE WEDDING was *more* than
a convenient solution!

Available this month In
The Bridal Collection
Only Make-Believe
by Bethany Campbell
Harlequin Romance #3230

Available wherever Harlequin books are sold.

HARLEQUIN ROMANCE®

Some people have the spirit
of Christmas all year round...

People like Blake Connors
and Karin Palmer.

Meet them—and love them!—in
Eva Rutland's
ALWAYS CHRISTMAS.

Harlequin Romance #3240
Available in December wherever
Harlequin books are sold.

HRHX

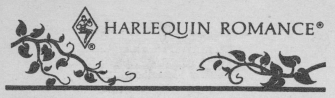

HARLEQUIN ROMANCE®

After her father's heart attack, Stephanie Bloomfield comes home to Orchard Valley, Oregon, to be with him and with her sisters.

Orchard Valley

Steffie learns that many things have changed in her absence—but not her feelings for journalist Charles Tomaselli. He was the reason she left Orchard Valley. Now, three years later, will he give her a reason to stay?

"The Orchard Valley trilogy features three delightful, spirited sisters and a trio of equally fascinating men. The stories are rich with the romance, warmth of heart and humor readers expect, and invariably receive, from Debbie Macomber."

—Linda Lael Miller

Don't miss the Orchard Valley trilogy by Debbie Macomber:

Look for the special cover flash on each book!

Available wherever Harlequin books are sold.

ORC-2

·HARLEQUIN· HISTORICAL

CHRISTMAS

·STORIES·1992·

Capture the magic and romance of Christmas in the 1800s with HARLEQUIN HISTORICAL CHRISTMAS STORIES 1992, a collection of three stories by celebrated historical authors. The perfect Christmas gift!

Don't miss these heartwarming stories, available in November wherever Harlequin books are sold:

MISS MONTRACHET REQUESTS by Maura Seger
CHRISTMAS BOUNTY by Erin Yorke
A PROMISE KEPT by Bronwyn Williams

Plus, as an added bonus, you can receive a FREE keepsake Christmas ornament. Just collect four proofs of purchase from any November or December 1992 Harlequin or Silhouette series novels, or from any Harlequin or Silhouette Christmas collection, and receive a beautiful dated brass Christmas candle ornament.